A REVIVED

MODERN

CLASSIC

THE SEA AND POISON

ALSO BY SHUSAKU ENDO

Deep River
The Final Martyrs
Five by Endo
The Girl I Left Behind
The Samurai
Stained Glass Elegies

SHUSAKU ENDO
THE SEA AND POISON

Translated by Michael Gallagher

A NEW DIRECTIONS BOOK

Manufactured in the United States of America
New Directions Books are printed on acid-free paper
First published as New Directions Paperbook 737 in 1992
Published by arrangement with Peter Owen Publishers, London

Library of Congress Cataloging-in-Publication Data

Endō, Shūsaku, 1923-
　　[Umi to dokuyaku. English]
　　The sea and poison / Shūsaku Endō ; translated by Michael Gallagher.
　　p.　　cm. — (A Revived modern classic) (New Directions
paperbook ; 737)
　　Translation of: Umi to dokuyaku.
　　ISBN 978-0-8112-1198-7
　　I.　Title.　　II.　Series.
PL849.N4U4513　　　1992
895.6'35 — dc20　　　　　　　　　　　　　　　　　　91-41413
　　　　　　　　　　　　　　　　　　　　　　　　　　　CIP

New Directions Books are published for James Laughlin
by New Directions Publishing Corporation
80 Eighth Avenue, New York 10011

EIGHTH PRINTING

CONTENTS

INTRODUCTION

Shusaku Endo came into prominence as a novelist in the mid-1950s. His reputation was firmly established in 1958 when *The Sea and Poison* won him the prestigious Akutagawa Prize. Besides writing novels, he is also a playwright, a journalist, a screen and television writer, and, with that busyness that for good or ill characterizes most Japanese writers, he appears on television frequently to comment on one thing or another and he writes a regular interview feature for a weekly magazine.

Endo was baptized as a Catholic while a very young schoolboy without thinking much about it or finding his new faith either particularly irksome or consoling. He entered Waseda, one of the most famous Japanese private universities, with the intention of studying medicine but eventually opted for French literature. After a short period of military service at the end of the War, he went to France for further study. During his stay in France, he was much impressed by the extent to which European traditions were rooted in Christianity and the significance it therefore had even for those Europeans who were no longer formal believers. He began to contrast this with the situation in his own land and with his own attitude towards Catholicism, a religion that had been, to use his own metaphor, not so much something that was a part of him but rather like a suit of clothes that he had put on.

According to the formulation of the perceptive American critic and translator, Francis Mathy, Endo like so many Japanese thinkers before, came to realize that the West 'is

1

informed by the Christian faith, even where it is formally rejected; the East, on the other hand, is informed by a kind of pantheism'. Cultural intercourse thus becomes a hazardous form of communication, and the Japanese writer who attempts to borrow from the West undergoes special risk. Pantheism knows no tension of opposites – between good and evil, flesh and spirit, God and the devil – such as is at the heart of the popular Christian life view. Such Japanese writers, therefore, according to Endo, have inevitably fastened upon one element, neglecting the other which is in tension with it, either ignoring the anti-thetical element completely or else interpreting it in such a weak fashion that it lacks sufficient strength to make for real conflict.

Apparently not much daunted by the alleged failure of so many of his countrymen, Endo chose not only to try to portray precisely this form of conflict but to set this conflict against the calm passivity of pantheism that he sees as the dominant Japanese religious mood. The following statement makes evident how deliberate was his decision and how much he realized the difficulty of the task that he had set himself:

> We can at least begin. . . . We can take our concave world without a God and contrast it as vigorously as possible with the Western convex world, which has known the existence of God. By 'vigorously' I mean that we must lay aside all methods of approach that foster the delusion that our concave world is really a convex one, a delusion that many writers even to our day have harboured. We must not think of the litera-ture of the Christian West as being in our own cultural stream, nor at the same time must we hold it off at a respectful distance, since it is this very thing,

2

so widely separated from us, that presses down most
heavily upon us.

In the three novels in which this 'vigorous contrast' is most
evidently at work, *Kiiroi Hito, Nanji mo mata,* and
Chinmoku, Endo's specific method is to set Japanese and
European characters against one another, Japanese and
Europeans who, for the most part, are 'afflicted' with each
other's culture.

Kiiroi Hito (Yellow Man, 1955), is written in the form of
a letter sent by Chiba, a young student no longer a practising Catholic, to his former pastor, Father Brou, a French
missionary. Much of the letter consists of passages from
the diary of another French priest, an apostate named
Duran, now dead, who was married to a woman named
Kimiko. Brou and Kimiko are the extremes, neither of
them taking enough notice of the other culture to be much
disturbed by it; whereas Duran and Chiba are Endo
people: those caught in the middle. In this novel they
seemed to have gained from their personal failures the
insight that 'yellow' and 'white' sensibilities are after all
fundamentally different and that any attempt to evangelize
the Japanese must end in failure. As persons Chiba and
Duran differ sharply, a difference, however, which underlies
the apparent validity of their insight. Chiba feels nothing
but a kind of general weariness and ennui because of his
loss of faith and his loveless affair with his cousin. The
apostate Duran is tormented by guilt and the fear of
damnation.

In *Nanji mo mata* (And Now You, 1965), Endo portrays
the other side of the coin in more detail: if the European
in Japan is up against an impossible task in attempting to
assimilate Japanese culture, so, too, is the Japanese in
Europe confronted with Western culture. The protagonist

3

is Tanaka, a young lecturer in French literature who goes to Paris for advanced studies. He returns disillusioned and worn out, convinced, furthermore, that this is as it should be, since any Japanese who came through the same experience still persuaded that he could assimilate Western culture would be too unperceptive to realize the enormity of the task.

Finally, in his famous *Chinmoku* (Silence) which won the *Tanizaki* Prize in 1966,* Endo portrays the conflict between Eastern and Western thought in highly dramatic terms. *Chinmoku*, like *The Sea and Poison,* is based upon an historical event, in this case, the apostasy of the seventeenth century Portuguese Jesuit Ferreira.

Since Ferreira was not an ordinary Jesuit but the provincial of the order in Japan, a man who had worked heroically for twenty years under the most trying circumstances, his apostasy under torture was a severe blow to the persecuted Christians, a shock that was aggravated when Ferreira, under what further pressure is not known, took a Japanese wife and cooperated with the Shogunate officials in the apprehending of Christians. Almost nothing is known of Ferreira's subsequent history, a circumstance that gives Endo ample scope.

In Endo's fictionalized version, the old apostate is confronted with a young Jesuit named Roderigo, a former student of his at the seminary in Coimbra, who had been captured soon after his arrival from Macao. Another main character in the novel is the governor of Nagasaki, Inoue, who questions the young Jesuit and tells him that his hopes of evangelizing Japan were empty ones because Japan is like a swamp which indeed draws anything and

*This novel was published under the title *Silence* in the English translation of William Johnston by Tuttle-Sophia University in 1969.

4

everything into itself but in the process changes it all intrinsically. Roderigo resists this line of argument, but when he hears the same from Ferreira, whom he had so much revered, it has much more cogency. Even the martyrs who seemed to have died so heroically for the faith that the foreign priests brought them, Ferreira argues, actually died for the sake of some vision all their own, only superficially related to what the Europeans had tried to teach them. Roderigo undergoes a crisis of faith, which he comes through still believing in Christ but no longer sure that the Church in which he had once placed such trust is actually able to speak to all men with wisdom and authority. He feels that Christ speaks to him – breaking the silence that gives the novel its title – and tells him to step upon the *fumie,* the bronze image of Christ used by the Shogunate officials to test suspected Christians and to formalize apostasy, because Christ himself would have done so in order to save from further suffering the poor, ignorant farmers whom the Jesuits have converted.

In an essay so brief, I cannot present anything like a critique of Endo's theme or his manner of developing and interpreting it. I think it might be of interest, however, to call to the reader's attention and to comment briefly upon the charge made against Endo's novels, particularly *Chinmoku,* by both native Christians and foreign missionaries. As Francis Mathy puts it, Endo exaggerates the conflict between the Eastern and Western religious outlooks and so stacks the cards against any possibility of rapprochement, even if, in the case of *Chinmoku,* he has to distort history to accomplish this.

This charge, I think, has some weight to it if one accepts its premise, something, however, that I cannot do because I feel that to do so involves confusing theology, philosophy, and history with literary criticism. Endo is a novelist,

5

after all, and one should judge him according to literary criteria, which, God knows, are exacting enough.

I mention this charge, however, not solely for the purpose of expressing my disagreement with it but rather because I think Endo's ability to provoke this kind of strong reaction tells something about him. It sharply differentiates him from writers such as Mishima, Tanizaki, and Kawabata. Graham Greene, who seems to have influenced Endo more than a little, once told a French interviewer that the writing of novels was something altogether different from the composition of religious tracts and so when he sat down to write, his sole concern was to turn out the best possible story. He would rather be known, therefore, as a writer who happened to be a Catholic than as a Catholic writer. These remarks were widely quoted by critics of every shade of belief and disbelief, and can, I think, shed light on Endo's own position. What followed, however, seems to have been generally overlooked: 'When one is a Catholic, everything that one writes is imbued with Catholicism.' And here, too, despite his own alleged thesis of never the twain, we have Endo.

Christianity, whatever validity it has as a religion and whatever validity religion itself has, for that matter, has at least provided a dramatic view of man as a free and therefore responsible creature put at the centre of the universe, a being capable of either damnation or salvation. It has been a view congenial to artistic inspiration, whatever the repression exercised by the Church herself, and it has, since Augustine's *Confessions*, stimulated or provoked the most intensely personal literature the world has ever known.

Whatever Endo's personal faith or lack of it, his artistic impulse is altogether Christian in the sense indicated above. He is quite taken up with the concept of freedom and

6

responsibility and altogether aware of the vital relationship that joins the two. Thus he cannot limit himself to a private universe of sex and sensibility as do most Japanese novelists but in his serious work he must, willy-nilly, deal with wider concerns capable of stirring public reactions. Thus Endo is the only major Japanese novelist who, in the novel that follows, has confronted the problem of individual responsibility in wartime.

Japanese novelists are unfortunate, I think, in that there are too few critics of insight and integrity to ride herd upon them, even though this is a misfortune that their British and American opposite numbers would no doubt envy them. Endo is still in his prime, and if he is willing to write at his best and curtail some of his activity, he is, I think, capable of achieving a position in world literature at least as high as some of his countrymen now far better known in the West.

The Sea and Poison, though it is a comparatively early work, should provide the reader with a sufficient basis to make some judgment of his own. Besides this English translation, incidentally, it has also been published in a Russian translation.

Finally, I would like to take this opportunity to express my gratitude to Dr Helen Li, Dr Mizuide Jun, and Dr Lu Shan-ta for reading the entire manuscript and offering many helpful suggestions.

Michael Gallagher

PART ONE

The Sea and Poison

PROLOGUE

In August, the hottest time of the year, I moved out here to this residential area called West Matsubara. The style 'residential area' is a caprice of the real estate agency. Since it takes over an hour to get here from Shinjuku Station in central Tokyo, the houses are few. A main highway passes the local station, stretching out with uncompromising straightness, and now the sun is beating down upon it with a relentless glare. Dump trucks are always going by hauling gravel from somewhere or other; and on the back of the trucks young labourers, towels twisted around their necks, sing popular songs, as one is doing now.

> When you sail, don't
> Pull up the anchor weeping.
> Be a man, do it laughing. . . .

The trucks stir dense clouds of dust every time they go by. And then as it settles, the shops on both sides of the road gradually loom into view once more. On the right are a tobacconist, a butcher, and a drugstore. On the left a noodle place and a gas station. And that's about all there is to it. Oh, but I forgot to mention that there's a clothing store too. It's all by itself, about fifty yards past the gas station. You wonder why the owner picked a spot like this, so far away from the city.

Thanks to the trucks, his Gentlemen's Clothing sign and his show window are both covered with a thick, chalky coat of dust. In the window is a flesh-coloured mannequin.

11

It's a rather unsettling figure, the kind of mannequin used in medical exhibits and the like. It represents just the torso of a man, a white man as it happens. From the red paint on his head, it seems that his creator's aim was to make him a redhead. So, with his long nose and his blue eyes, he smiles all day long – an enigmatic smile.

When I moved here, we were in the midst of a long, unpleasant dry spell. The field between the noodle shop and the gas station was parched and cracked, and in the shrivelled stalks of corn, katydids complained of the drought's affliction.

'This heat's awful. I think I'll go and take a bath, but it's pretty far, isn't it?' my wife said.

To get to the bathhouse, you had to walk about four hundred yards down the highway past the station.

'Yes, but at least there *is* a bathhouse. There isn't a doctor, and I've got to have this lung treated every week.'

The next day my wife found a doctor's surgery. She said that she had seen a doctor's plate hanging in front of a place close to the bathhouse. Last year when we all had our chests X-rayed at my company, a small cavity had shown up in the upper part of my left lung. Fortunately, the pleura had not been infected, and I was able to get by without having my rib cut; but I had been receiving pneumothorax treatments for over half a year before moving here. So now I had to find a new doctor as soon as possible.

In order to locate this Dr Suguro's surgery, I went looking for the street my wife had told me about. The windows of the bathhouse reflected the bright afternoon sun. Evidently the local farming families were already inside taking their baths, for I could hear faintly but distinctly the noise of splashing water and the knocking of wooden buckets. A happy sound, I thought with a sudden unwonted nostalgia.

12

I soon found the doctor's surgery, just behind the bath-house and separated from it by a field of ripe red tomatoes. It was a small, shabbily constructed house, more like a shed than a surgery. There was nothing at all that could be called a fence. Some brown shrubbery, blasted by the sun, served as a border facing the tomato field. It was still well before sunset. Why, then, I wondered, does he have his wooden shutters closed already? In the garden lay a child's dirty red boot. A pathetic dog kennel stood near the door, but there was no sign of a dog. I rang the bell a number of times, but there was no answer. Finally I walked round to the garden. Then one of the shutters opened a bit, and the face of a man who was wearing a white medical coat appeared.

'Who are you?'

'Well, I'm a patient.'

'What do you mean?'

'What I'd like to do is get some pneumothorax treatments.'

'Pneumothorax?'

The doctor seemed to be a man of about forty or so. He stared vacantly at me, incessantly rubbing his chin with his right hand. Perhaps because the house faced away from the setting sun, the room with its shuttered windows was forebodingly dark; and in the thick shadow the man's face seemed greyish and oddly bloated.

'You've been to a doctor before, I suppose?'

'Yes. For half a year I've been getting this treatment.'

'You have an X-ray?'

'Well, yes, but I left it at the house.'

'Can't do anything without the X-ray.'

And with that he closed the shutter again. For a moment I stood there staring, but not the slightest sound came from the house.

13

'A funny kind of doctor,' I said that night to my wife. 'He's really a funny kind of doctor.'

'Oh, I suppose he has his regular patients.'

'May be so. But besides he talks with some kind of accent. He hasn't lived in Tokyo very long. He comes from somewhere else.'

'Well, anyway, you'd better get your lung taken care of before you go to Kyushu. My sister's wedding is pretty close now, in September.'

'Yes.'

But I didn't go to Dr Suguro's surgery the next day or the day after that. My breathing gradually started to become painful as the volume of air taken into my left lung diminished little by little. In the pneumothorax treatment, air is pumped into the side in order to diminish the pleural cavity pressing on the lung. The needle used to insert it is a huge thick one, about the size of a darning needle, which is tipped with rubber. It's not the insertion of the needle that bothers me so much in this process, but it's the place where they have to place it. The needle is inserted into the lower side. Now this is a spot which by nature your arm covers and protects. The moment when I have to raise my arm and wait for the needle, I feel – why I don't know – a chilling numbness grip my side. Part of it, of course, comes from the uneasiness resulting from having to raise my arm and to expose myself in such a defenceless way.

To get the needle from a doctor to whom you are accustomed to going is unpleasant enough. A strange doctor, therefore, is all the more unsettling. Sometimes, if the doctor is clumsy, a spontaneous pneumothorax develops, often resulting in the death of the patient by asphyxiation. And so when I recalled Dr Suguro sticking that grey, bloated face of his out from behind the shutters, the room beyond him in sinister shadow, my desire to go faded away.

14

But be that as it may, you can't be forever thinking about yourself. My sister-in-law's wedding in Fukuoka, down in Kyushu, was only two weeks away; and since my wife was pregnant and couldn't make the trip, I had to go in her place. My sister-in-law's parents were dead, which left no one but me to hold up her side of the affair.

O.K., I told myself, get the X-ray and let's go. But I brooded over the 'let's go' for two or three more days.

In the meantime, I made my first appearance at the local bathhouse. Since it was a Saturday, I had come home from work about two in the afternoon. So many trucks had passed while I was walking along the road that I was covered with grey dust from head to foot. Probably because it was so early, there was only one man there ahead of me. He was a shrewd-faced individual, and he was lolling in the water, loosely gripping the edge of the bath with his hands, his chin resting upon them. After looking in my direction for a while, he spoke.

'The water's really nice about now, isn't it?'

'Huh?'

'The water's nice now, isn't it? You come later, and the farmer's kids around here have got it all dirty. The little bastards even piss in it. Damn them.'

As I washed my thin arms and chest over in the corner, not wanting to make a display of myself, I noticed that this was the owner of the gas station. He had always been wearing a white uniform and handling a pump, so I hadn't recognized him until now. The sound of children crying came from the women's side of the bathhouse.

With a noisy flourish, he lifted himself up out of the water. His shrewd face looked back from the wall mirror.

'All right! Let's get down to it!' Then he sat down on an upturned wooden bucket and began to wash his long legs.

15

'You been in this area only a little while, uh?'

'It's been a week. I hope we'll be good neighbours.'

'What kind of work do you do?'

'I work for a nail wholesaler.'

'Your company's in Tokyo, uh? Having to go there every day's a pain in the ass, I suppose.'

Covertly I took in his chest, its light skin protected from the sun by his underwear. His ribs were somewhat prominent, but his well-knit bone structure gave his body a certain power. Puny men like me are afflicted with a painful feeling of inferiority when confronted with a man with a strong physique. On his right shoulder, there was a scar about two inches or so in diameter, apparently the result of a burn. The taut, twisted flesh had the shape of a ragged blossom.

'It looks like your wife's pregnant.'

'Yes.'

'I saw her walking down to the station the other day. Looked like she was having a pretty hard time of it.'

'Is there a doctor around here anywhere?' I thought I'd see if there were anyone besides Dr Suguro. My own lung trouble and my wife's pregnancy were beginning to weigh upon me more and more.

'Why there's Dr Suguro. His surgery is right behind here.'

'How is he?'

'Not bad at all, according to what they say. Never opens his mouth. Funny sort of guy.'

'Funny, huh?'

'Doesn't bother you about his bill at all. Even if you forget all about it, he wouldn't say a word.'

'I went there the other day, and he had the shutters closed.'

'That's probably because his wife took the kid and went

to Tokyo. They say she used to be a nurse.'

'Been here long?'

'Who?'

'The doctor.'

'I don't think so. I think he came a little before I did.'

Dirty grey water flowed from around his feet. As he lathered himself his right elbow kept jabbing close to my face. Red with tingling blood, his toughened flesh took on the sleek sheen of an otter beneath the soap and water. Envy flicked within me. The burn I spoke of before on his right arm had now become a sodden white.

'Is it a burn, that?'

'What, this? This is from a trench mortar. It was in China. The chinks gave it to me. It's a wound to be proud of.'

'I suppose it hurt a lot?'

'Oh, it did and it didn't. Think of a red-hot iron bar, see? Then, wham! You're hit with it. That's the sort of feeling. You drafted?'

'Uh, just at the end of the war. I was back home right away.'

'Oh, I see. Then you got no idea about something like the sound of those chink mortars. Whoosh, whoosh, whoosh! In they'd come whistling. That was something.'

I thought of the training regiment to which I had been assigned. In the dimly lit orderly rooms had sat any number of shrewd-faced men like the gas station owner. While they were berating us recruits, their cruel, narrow eyes would glitter with unmistakable pleasure. Perhaps now these men, too, were gas station owners somewhere.

'But we had our fun in China too. Did whatever we wanted with the women. Any bastard that made any complaints we tied to a tree and used for target practice.'

'Women?'

'No! Men.'

As he soaped his head, he turned towards me. For the first time apparently, he noticed my scrawny chest and thin arms, and his face took on an incredulous expression.

'Pretty skinny, aren't you? Why you could stab some-body with one of those arms. You wouldn't have made it as a soldier. My kind. . . .' He paused for a moment. 'Of course, I'm not the only one. There's one or two here of the bunch that did their bit in China. There's me and the guy that owns that men's wear store – you know it, don't you?' He laughed abruptly. 'He really raised hell in Nan-king, I think. The bastard was an M.P.'

A radio somewhere was playing a popular song. It was Hibari Misora singing it. From the women's side of the bathhouse came the sound of crying children again. I dried myself.

'Well, excuse me. I'm going.'

In the dressing room a man with his back turned was taking off his shirt. It was Dr Suguro. He looked at me blinking but averted his gaze at once. Did he remember the incident of the other day or didn't he? The afternoon sun struck the doctor's forehead, which was covered with tiny beads of sweat. As I returned home, I passed through the tomato field. On all sides the katydids sang in a hoarse, rasping pitch which grated upon my ears. While going by the men's wear shop, I stopped all at once. I had been thinking of what the gas station owner had told me. As before a layer of dust covered the window. Inside the shop a man was at work bent over a sewing machine. His eyes were sunken and his cheekbones prominent. Was this the man who had been a military policeman in Nanking? Then as I thought a bit, I knew that I had seen many faces like his too. In the orderly rooms of the training regiments, this type of farmer's face had been common enough among the veterans.

'Can I help you?'

'No, no! It's just that it's so hot.' I was flustered. 'It's really awful isn't it? Is that a job you're working on?'

'No!' He laughed with unexpected affability. 'A job to work on! Out here? Not much chance of that.'

In the window the mannequin kept smiling his enigmatic smile. The two blue eyes stared fixedly into space.

After taking such trouble to go to the bathhouse, I came back home dripping with sweat. I sat down on the porch next to my wife, embracing her with my hands resting on her swollen stomach.

'Say, you know about the sphinx?'

'What's that?'

'You know that men's wear place by the cornfield? There's a dummy in the window. When the sun's going down, it shines in there, you see. And when I see that faint, mocking smile, I can't help thinking of the Egyptian desert and the sphinx.'

'Why don't you stop thinking about the Egyptian desert and be quick about getting to the doctor?'

Since my wife hadn't left any room for argument, that evening I took the X-ray picture and went to Dr Suguro's. The shutters were still closed, the child's boot, as I had more than half expected, still lay in the garden, and the dog kennel was empty as before. Evidently Dr Suguro did his own cooking while his wife was away.

The inside of the house and the examination room too were filled with an odour of general uncleanliness. Was it the accumulated odour of all the patients who had preceded me, or was it the smell of some sort of medicine? I couldn't tell. The white curtain covering the window was torn in the middle, and half of it had been turned yellow

19

by the sun. I noticed with an unpleasant twinge that there was a small spot of blood on Dr Suguro's white coat. As I lay on a creaky bed, he held the X-ray up in front of his nose, studying it with blinking eyes.

'I was getting 400 c.c. of air from my last doctor.'

Dr Suguro didn't respond. I looked fixedly at him as he took a glass bottle containing the pneumothorax needle from a drawer of his desk, examined the hole at its tip, inserted it into the rubber tube, and prepared the anaesthetic shot. His thick, hairy fingers moved like caterpillars. There was dirt packed under the fingernails.

'Raise your arm,' he ordered me in a low voice.

His fingers probed my side for the spot between the two rib bones. He was making sure of the place to insert the needle. There was a cold, metallic chillness to that touch. More than that, there was an impersonal, unfeeling competency to it which seemed to deal with me not as a patient but as some sort of laboratory specimen.

'The other doctor wasn't like this.' I suddenly began to shudder with that instinct belonging to a patient. 'The other fellow had some warmth.'

Just at that moment the needle entered my side. I distinctly felt it resting between the thorax and the rib membrane. The doctor's technique had been remarkable.

'Ah!' I sighed with relief.

Dr Suguro gave no sign that he had heard but gazed out of the window. He was thinking about something else, it seemed, something which had nothing to do with me or with my affairs. 'Close-mouthed and a bit odd' had been the verdict of the gas station owner. And indeed Dr Suguro was a bit odd.

'No sociability, that's all. There's a lot of doctors like that,' my wife said.

'Mmm . . . but still. . . . The way he put the needle in.

You don't find that in a country doctor, you see. I wonder what he's doing living in a place like this.'

Putting a pneumothorax needle into a patient's side might seem like nothing special, but I had heard from the old doctor I used to go to when I lived in Kyodo, that it was an extremely difficult thing to do.

'You can't trust a young intern to do it. Getting the needle in in just the right way takes an experienced, practised doctor.'

This old doctor, someone had told me, had worked for a long time in a tuberculosis sanatorium. One day he gave me a thorough explanation of the whole process. If the needle is new, there's no chance of any pain, but to put an old needle with a dull tip into the pleura painlessly and quickly, just the right application of force is necessary. As I said before, there's the possibility of an attack of spontaneous pneumothorax; and even if this doesn't occur, if the needle doesn't penetrate to precisely the right spot with a single thrust, the patient will have a painful time of it. Then, too, speaking from my own experience, even this veteran doctor in Kyodo would slip up once or twice a month and have to withdraw the needle to try again. At times like that, I was seized with pain as though my side had been ripped open.

This never happened with Dr Suguro. With one thrust he would insert the needle quickly and surely right between the pleura and the lung, lodging it there securely. There was no pain at all. It was done before I could even flinch. If what the old doctor in Kyodo had said was true, then it seemed that this man with the grey, bloated face had, somewhere or other, gained a considerable amount of medical skill. If he were so capable a doctor, there should have been no need for him to settle in a barren spot like this, so lacking in every attractive feature. Yet he had come. Why, I wondered.

21

However, despite all his skill, I still felt uneasy about him. More than uneasiness, distaste. Every time I felt the touch of those hard fingers probing my ribs, the chilling metallic touch so difficult to describe, that indefinite but powerful instinct for life common to all patients shuddered inside me. I thought that I felt this way merely because the movement of his thick fingers was so suggestive of a cluster of caterpillars, but there was more to it than that.

A month had now passed since we had moved here. At the end of September I had to go to Kyushu for my sister-in-law's wedding. My wife's stomach had swollen so that her pregnancy was quite obvious.

'It's wide, so maybe it's a girl,' she murmured happily, brushing a fold of her maternity dress against her cheek. 'She just kicked! Sometimes she kicks me.'

The gas station owner, in his white uniform as usual, walked about in front of his pumps. I'd say hello to him on the way to work. Sometimes I'd stop, and we'd talk for a bit about nothing at all. At the bathhouse I'd meet not only him but also the men's wear proprietor. Since even my sickness was getting better, I thought of myself as happy. Soon there'd be a baby. I had my own house, small though it was. This amounted to no more than an ordinary kind of happiness, perhaps, but what was wrong with that, I thought.

But still, this matter of Dr Suguro stirred my curiosity. Hadn't his wife come back yet? The shutters, as always, stayed shut. Had the child's red rubber boot in the garden been carried off by the dog, if there were a dog? Some time or other it disappeared.

One day I picked up just a bit of information about him. This occurred about the fifth time that I went to him for treatment. I was waiting my turn outside the examination room when I found in an old magazine a programme for the graduation ceremony of Fukuoka University Medical School. The name Suguro is not a common one, so it took me just a moment to satisfy myself that my doctor was indeed listed there. What was rather a coincidence was that my sister-in-law's wedding was taking place in Fukuoka at the end of the month.

'The accent is Fukuoka, in Kyushu,' I declared to my wife.

'What accent?'

'His. The first day I went there, when he told me he couldn't help me without the X-rays. The way he said it.'

Since both my wife and I had been born in Tokyo, we had no idea whether the accent was Western; but since my imitation sounded amusing, we both laughed.

'I'll bet the wife's run out on him,' the gas station owner was speculating in the bathhouse. 'Anyway, they say he's got himself another nurse.'

'A funny sort of fellow.'

'Yes, he's funny, but that's all right with me. My kid got sick last year. He examined him and he hasn't asked for his fee yet.'

'The wife who may have run off, what kind of woman was she?'

'Her? Like her husband, bad complexion. Hardly showed her face at all and you'd never see her going to the station.'

Each time I went to his surgery for my treatment, Dr Suguro hardly had a word to say. Day by day the torn curtain yellowed more and more in the sun, but it was left just as it was. Most of the patients were farmers' wives and children. They'd sit on the step outside the door, leafing through the old newspapers and magazines put out for them, and wait their turns with untiring patience. Since there was no nurse, Dr Suguro himself had to take care of preparing the medicine.

One September evening, still heavy with the torrid heat of summer, I was walking aimlessly along the highway when I happened to catch sight of Dr Suguro standing beside the road with a cane. He was staring into the window of the men's wear store. When he noticed me approaching, the doctor averted his gaze and abruptly walked on. When I bowed he gave only a nod. The window had its usual layer of dust. The owner was nowhere to be seen. The white, supposedly red-headed mannequin stared at me with his thin, mocking smile. It was this sphinx that Dr Suguro had been staring at so earnestly.

At the end of September, I headed for Fukuoka in Kyushu, a long tedious train journey away, for my sister-in-law's wedding. Before leaving, I had gone for another treatment, but I hadn't said anything to him about the trip. There is not much point in discussing something with somebody if he never bothers to give you anything resembling an answer.

My sister-in-law had settled upon a 'love marriage' with someone who worked in the same office as her in Tokyo. His family's home was in Fukuoka, and so they decided to have the wedding there. For my sister-in-law, who was rather alone in the world, I would be the only relative in attendance; and so I felt I was taking on a burden I was hardly equal to.

I intended to stay overnight in Fukuoka before returning to Tokyo. I had heard that it was a city with many rivers, but its main one turned out to be murky and to have a ditch odour about it. I saw the body of a dead puppy and a rubber shoe floating in it. I thought of the odour of Dr Suguro's garden and examination room. Then, too, the local people spoke with the same accent as him. When he had been a medical student, he must have looked at this river, walked through this town. A strange way for my thoughts to be running.

The wedding reception was held at a small restaurant in the centre of town. My sister-in-law's husband was a short, apparently good-natured office worker. Like me he was one of the mass of commuters who wait every morning on the platforms of Shinjuku Station. How nice if after a while my sister-in-law had a child and settled down with this young man in a house in a not very expensive suburb somewhere, to enjoy an ordinary sort of happiness. Nothing special, nothing to rave about, but as I watched the two of them, my thoughts drifting in no particular direction, it seemed to me that the ordinary can give one the greatest happiness.

Seated beside me at the table was a man who said that he was a cousin of the bridegroom. He too was short, but thickset. He gave me his card, and I noticed M.D. on it.

'Did you graduate from Fukuoka University?' I asked him. Since there wasn't much to talk about, I happened to think of the programme I had come across in Dr Suguro's surgery. 'Did you happen to know a medical student named Suguro, Doctor?'

'Suguro, Suguro. . . .' My companion tilted his head to one side. One or two glasses of saké had turned his face quite red. 'You mean Jiro Suguro?'

'That's the one.'

'Suguro. Do you know him?'

'He's my doctor. I get treatment for my lung from him.'

'Oh. . . .' For some time he studied my face. 'So now he's in Tokyo, you say. Imagine that.'

'You were a friend in college? Of Dr Suguro's?'

'No. He. . . . Maybe you know and maybe you don't know; but anyway what happened was what usually happens in a case like that.' He lowered his voice at once and began his story.

When the reception was over, my sister-in-law and her husband left for the station. The relatives and I saw them off there. Rain had begun to fall throughout the city. As soon as the honeymooners had departed, everyone began to feel ill at ease. The family invited me to a restaurant with them; but I told them I was tired, and I returned to my inn. There were scarcely any guests there. After the chambermaid had laid out my bedding, I sat for a long time cross-legged, thinking – thinking and smoking one cigarette after another. After I had slipped under the thick, quilted spread, I couldn't sleep. I kept on thinking about what the bridegroom's cousin at the reception had told me about Dr Suguro in such a stealthy voice. I could hear the sound of falling rain on the roof. From somewhere far away inside the hotel a group of maids with nothing to do were laughing and talking.

If I dozed off, I soon awoke. In the darkness the image of Dr Suguro would loom up and disappear again and again, his grey, puffy face, his thick caterpillar fingers. Once more I felt the chilling touch of those fingers on the skin of my right side.

There was more rain the next day. In the afternoon I went out in the midst of it to visit a newspaper office in the city.

'Excuse me, but I was wondering if it would be all right to take a look at some back numbers of your paper.'

The girl at the receptionist's desk gave me a suspicious look, but she put through a call to the archives for me.

'An article from about what time?'

'Right after the War. There was a trial wasn't there, about the vivisections at Fukuoka Medical School?' I asked.

'Do you have any kind of authorization?'

'No, no, nothing like that.'

Finally I got the necessary permission. In a corner of the third floor archives, I read through the back numbers covering that period for about an hour. It was the affair involving the staff of the Medical School during the War. Eight captured American airmen had been used for medical experiments. In general the purpose of the experiments had been to obtain such information as how much blood a man could lose and remain alive, how much salt water in place of blood could safely be injected into a man's veins, and up to what point a man could survive the excision of lung tissue. There were twelve medical personnel involved in the vivisections, two of them nurses. The trial opened in Fukuoka but was later transferred to Yokohama. Towards the end of the list of defendants, I found Dr Suguro's name. There was nothing in the articles about his part in the experiments. The professor of medicine who had been in charge of the experiments committed suicide at the first opportunity. The principal defendants received long prison terms. Three, however, got off with light sentences of two years. Dr Suguro was one of the latter.

From the window of the newspaper office, I looked out at the clouds, the colour of soiled cotton wool, which hung low over the city. From time to time I'd look up from the articles to gaze at that dark sky. I left the newspaper office and walked through the streets. The thin, slanting rain struck my face. The passing cars, buses, lorries and street-cars made the same noises as they did in Tokyo. Young girls in raincoats of red and blue and other vivid shades walked along the sidewalk, which was streaming with rain. From

27

the coffee shops came the sound of pleasant, titillating music. The singer Chiemi Eri was soon coming to town it seemed. Her face with its open, laughing mouth lent gaudy colour to the front of a cinema.

'Hey, Mister! How about a lottery ticket?' A woman in a full length apron accosted me from a doorway.

I felt tired and somehow out of sorts. I dropped into a coffee shop and had some coffee and a roll. Parents with their children and young men with their girl-friends came and went in and out through the door. I saw among them shrewd, long, narrow faces like that of the gas station owner. And square-jawed farmer faces with prominent cheek bones like that of the men's wear proprietor were frequent enough too. What was the gas station owner doing now, about this time of day? In his white uniform, was he filling the tank of a truck? Behind his dust covered show window, was the men's wear proprietor bent over his sewing machine? When one thought of it, both of them alike were men with murder in their pasts. So even in this West Matsubara to which I had moved, no matter how few its shops and houses, I had got to know two men who had tasted the experience of killing a man. And I could count Dr Suguro as a third.

Something, somehow, I could not figure out. How strange, I thought, that up to today, I had hardly reflected at all upon this. Now, this father of a family coming in through the door, perhaps during the War he killed a man or two. But now his face as he sips his coffee and scolds his children is not the face of a man fresh from murder. Just as with the show window in West Matsubara, past which the trucks rumble, the dust of the years settles on our faces too.

I left the shop and got on a streetcar. Fukuoka University Medical School was the stop at the end of the line.

28

A light rain had begun to fall again, and water was dripping from the pagoda trees which stood in neatly ordered ranks across the wide campus.

I soon found the wing containing the First Surgical Department, where the vivisection had been performed. Pretending to be someone visiting a patient, I climbed to the third floor. Up to the third floor, the wing consisted entirely of wards. In the corridors the smell of grime mingled with the permeating odour of disinfectant. There could be no doubt about it. This is what I had smelled in Dr Suguro's examination room – the same odour coming from the same poisonous source.

No one was in the operating theatre. Two leather-covered operating tables had been rolled over next to the window ledge. I squatted down on the floor and remained still for some time. Why I had come all the way up here I myself didn't know. I was thinking that somewhere in this dark room, some years before, Dr Suguro's grey, bloated face had had its due place. All at once I realized with a shock of surprise that I wanted to see him here.

I felt the start of a headache, so I went up to the roof. Fukuoka seemed to be crouching before me like a huge grey beast. Beyond the city I could see the ocean. The sea was a piercingly vivid blue, which I could feel, even at that distance, blurring my vision.

It was already autumn when I returned to Tokyo. I didn't tell my wife anything of course, and the next evening I went to Dr Suguro's. As he was fitting the needle into the rubber tube, I remarked in an offhand way: 'I just got back from a trip to Fukuoka.'

For an instant Dr Suguro looked at my face, but his habitual melancholy expression was as always. After that he began to probe my rib bones with his fingers. The spot of blood stood out on his white coat.

'Let me have an anaesthetic shot please!'

Ordinarily there was no need to use anaesthetic for someone like me, who had been getting treatment for nearly a year. But when I felt the cold touch of his fingers and saw the bloodstain on his coat, I cried out despite myself. After I had, I was struck by the thought that on the day of the vivisections, the American prisoners must have pleaded in the same way on the operating table.

Either because the sun had almost set or because the curtain was closed, the room, I felt, was gradually growing even darker than usual. I could hear the sound made by the air being pumped into my lungs as it bubbled through the water tank. My forehead was covered with sweat.

When the needle had been taken out of me, I felt a distinct surge of relief. Dr Suguro had his back turned and was writing something on a card, but all at once, blinking his eyes, he began to mutter something in a small, weary voice.

'. . . Because nothing could be done. At that time nothing could be done. From now on, I'm not sure at all. If I were caught in the same way, I might, I might just do the same thing again. The same thing. . . .'

I left his surgery and walked along the road, dragging my steps. The highway stretching so straight before me – I couldn't help wondering how far it went. A truck came towards me stirring up its dense clouds of dust. I stepped into the shelter offered by the men's wear shop to wait for it to pass. The mannequin was smiling his glazed smile.

'Four feet in the morning, two at midday, three in the evening – that's man.' I thought again of the riddle of the sphinx which I had heard in childhood. What should I do from now on: keep on going to Dr Suguro or not, I wondered.

1

'What time is the Old Man's round changed to?'

'Three-thirty.'

'Still in conference?'

'Yes.'

'Ah, what a world we're in here! Everybody wants to be Dean of the Medical School.'

The February wind whistled at the broken window. The paper which had been spread over the glass as a protection against the force of bomb blasts had worked loose in the wind which was beating a tattoo against the pane. Number Three Laboratory was on the north side of the wing so that, even though the time was only a little past two in the afternoon, the room was as dark and chilly as though it were evening.

On top of his desk, Toda had spread out some newspaper, and over it he was scraping a lump of dextrose with an old scalpel. After scraping a bit, he would gather some of the white crystals in his palm and with a great show of frugality lick them up.

After spreading some yellow sputum on a glass slide with a thin sliver of platinum, Suguro was drying it over a blue gas flame. The disagreeable smell of the heated sputum struck his nose.

'Ah, there's not enough carbol-fuchsin.'

'What?'

'The carbol-fuchsin's running out.'

When talking with his fellow intern Toda, Suguro would frequently use a few words of Osaka dialect. This had been a custom with them ever since they had become classmates

31

in college. In the past it had been a tacit symbol of their friendship.

'Who's sputum is that?'

'The old lady's,' Suguro answered, his face reddening. For he could feel Toda turning his gaze towards him, an ironic, mocking smile forming on his lips, around which there still clung a few particles of dextrose.

'Is that right? Still at it, eh?' said Toda, feigning great surprise. 'Why don't you give up on it? You're always going to extra trouble for that welfare case.'

'It doesn't take any trouble. None at all.'

'Whatever you do, she's a dead duck, isn't she? It's just a waste of carbol.'

But Suguro, blinking, began to smear the sputum. Scorched by the flame, the old lady's phlegm developed a brown rim like a fried egg. Looking at the glass slide, Suguro was reminded of her thin, shrivelled arms, which were brown in just the same way. Toda was right. The woman would last for no more than ten months. Each morning for a long time now, when he came into the unpleasant smelling ward, he noticed that the light in the old lady's eyes was gradually fading as she lay there on the dirty bed. She was a patient who, when Moji had been devastated by an air raid, had fled to Fukuoka hoping to be helped by her sister. But there she had been told that her sister's family was listed as missing. The police then sent her here to the University Hospital as a welfare patient, and since her arrival she had done nothing but lie in the Ward of Number Three Wing.

Since the disease had wasted away half her lungs, there was no way of saving her. The Old Man, Dr Hashimoto, had long since given up all hope.

'I think there's a chance maybe something can be done.'

'Something can be done?' Toda suddenly burst out in an

exasperated tone. 'Cut the sentimentality! Do something for one and so what? Look, the wards and the private rooms are filled with poor bastards who don't have a chance. Why this fascination with one old lady?'

'I'm not fascinated with her.'

'She reminds you of Mama, I suppose?'

'Not at all.'

'Ah, what a gentle lad you are! Your mind runs in the same track as that of these student nurses.'

Suguro's face reddened despite himself, as though an intimate secret had been brought to light; and with an offended air he threw the glass slide to the back of the shelf. How far Toda's description was true he didn't know. 'It's because she's my very first patient,' he said to himself, but he still felt embarrassment. 'I don't like seeing her there every morning in the ward, with that yellowed hair she has. Just seeing those hands of hers like chicken legs is unpleasant enough.' To confess as much was painful. He felt the sharp cutting edge of Toda's sarcasm. There's no room, Toda had said, for pity in a doctor in a world such as this. For it would do no good at all and could, in fact, do harm.

'Today everybody's on the way out.' His companion wrapped the dextrose in a piece of newspaper and put it in the desk. 'The poor bastard who doesn't die in the hospital gets his chance every night to die in an air raid. What's the point, then, of pitying one old lady. You'd be doing better to think of a new way of curing TB.'

Toda took his white coat from a hook on the wall and, giving Suguro the benefit of a fraternal, elder admonishing younger smile, walked out of the room with it over his arm.

It was already three. From the noise it seemed that the after lunch quiet period had ended. Once again the corri-

33

dors echoed with the noise of nurses scurrying to and fro. The patients who did their own cooking were splashing water at the sinks. In the broken window the college campus was framed, and he could see a car slowly climbing the road from the city. The car stopped in front of the main gate of Second Surgery, and a short, fat man in civilian clothes accompanied by a medical cadet climbed into it. As soon as the door was shut, the car started up and sped down the grey road, quickly passing out of sight. Such brisk movement on the deserted late-afternoon campus certainly clashed with the dark laboratory, the shabby hospital rooms, and the patients who lay in them. It was like a manifestation from another world.

'That was Dr Kando and the intern Kobori, I suppose. Then the conference must be over,' thought Suguro, a thought that plunged him deeper into melancholy. 'Conferences always mean a headache for us. The Old Man's going to spring something on us again.'

A month before, the Dean of the University Medical School, Dr Osugi, had collapsed with a brain haemorrhage. It had happened at a conference of medical officers of the Western Command and officials of the Ministry of Education. In the middle of a meeting, the old man got up, tottering a bit, and went to the toilet. A few moments later, there was a thud, and everyone came running to find him sitting on the floor, leaning against the wall with his face upturned. He was gripping the flush chain tenaciously.

Suguro remembered the funeral ceremony on the campus of the Medical School. It had been a cloudy, cold afternoon. The wind blowing in from the sea stirred up grey dust, and the scraps of newspapers scattered over the grounds, into little whirlwinds and made the canopy set up for the funeral flap furiously. In front of the canopy were the chairs for the high-ranking officers of the Western

34

Command, imposing figures who sat, legs arrogantly spread, with white gloved hands gripping their sword hilts. Opposite them sat the medical faculty. Perhaps it was because of their civilian clothes that they cut such poor figures; but at any rate they all wore bitter, weary expressions and looked thoroughly haggard and shabby.

An officer delivered an interminable speech before a photograph of the deceased, elucidating for the benefit of the medical students every nuance of the Way of True Loyalty which they, too, were to tread.

Even Suguro, though no more than a mere intern, nevertheless, just from seeing day after day the irascible expression on the face of the Old Man, Dr Hashimoto, was able to sense the anxious concern gripping the senior doctors swirling in orbit around the vacant chair of Dean of Medicine. Recently, while making his examination rounds and on similar occasions the Old Man had been unusually sharp with his assistants and quick to scold the welfare patients.

As Toda put it, the greater part of the medical faculty was under the sway of Dr Kando, Chief Surgeon of Second Surgery. From the point of view of age and of experience within the hospital, Toda and Suguro's 'Old Man', Dr Hashimoto, was by all odds the logical choice to succeed to the post of Dean of Medicine. However, the activity of the Kando faction made the outcome less assured. For some time now they had been strengthening their position in conjunction with the Western Command in Fukuoka. This story, too, came from Toda, and according to it Dr Kando had contracted secretly with the Army to turn over two wings of the hospital for the exclusive care of wounded soldiers if he became Dean of Medicine. The man who acted as the tireless liaison officer between Kando and the military was the intern Kobori, who worked as an instructor in Second Surgery.

An intern like Suguro, working at the lower levels, had no way of comprehending all aspects of the complicated state of affairs within the University. Though he did understand something of the situation, he had no inkling whatsoever that what would emerge from it would have a profound effect upon his own future.

'I'm not going to be a great man. That's for Dr Asai or Toda. They'll stay here at the University,' he thought. 'I'll go to a sanatorium in the mountains somewhere and work as a TB doctor. That'll be good enough. I'll be drafted soon, so I'll be leaving here.'

In the early evening, drab olive cars were perpetually stopping in front of the entrance of Second Surgery. Two medical cadets, green lapel insignia affixed to their uniform jackets, unaccustomed swords clacking against their boots, opened the door of one car and squat Dr Kando got in with an air of grave composure. The sight was enough to plunge Suguro into deep depression. For here was the source of the Old Man's irascibility and imperious severity during his ward rounds.

This afternoon, too, the Old Man's mood was a cause of worry for Suguro. When the time came for the three-thirty ward round, he was waiting outside the chief surgeon's office for the Old Man and Miss Oba, the chief nurse, to come out. With him were Toda and Asai, another intern. Suguro turned blinking to Asai, who, his rimless glasses flashing, was thumbing through a bundle of charts, and asked in a timid voice: 'I wonder what the conference was about?'

'I don't know.' Asai stared hard at him, as though implying that a mere intern had no business sticking his nose into the affairs of the Medical School. 'By the way, my friend,

I'm still waiting for that report on Mitsu Abé's stomach fluid. If the Old Man asks for it today, what then?'

This intern had just returned to the University as a reserve officer, and he was making use of the opportunity the situation presented to consolidate his position in First Surgery. Interns and young instructors were both swallowed up by the military, leaving the laboratories deserted; and in such circumstances, it was sensible of Dr Asai to consolidate his position. According to a rumour current in the hospital, he was engaged to the Old Man's niece.

Stammering, Suguro tried to defend himself; but the other with an expression of annoyance turned away and once again began an industrious perusal of his charts.

It was about four o'clock. The pale winter sunshine was fading from the corridors. The Old Man, accompanied by Chief Nurse Oba, who served as his secretary, at last appeared from inside the office. Both of them seemed extremely tired. The Old Man's green tie was askew at the neck of his white jacket. His usually neatly arranged silver hair seemed damp with sweat, and one or two hairs were plastered to his forehead. Only a few weeks ago, such negligence would have been unthinkable.

Suguro recalled that the Old Man had fallen in love with the German woman who was now his wife when he had been a student in Europe. 'Nothing like that would ever happen to a country boy like me,' he reflected unhappily.

'He's testy about something today too,' Toda whispered to Suguro as they walked beside each other down the corridor, following the Old Man, who had said not a word to them. 'Did you really check Mitsu Abé's stomach fluid?'

'Well, I was going to but. . . .' Suguro answered frowning. 'You've got to use the tube with her and it causes her a lot of pain. It's really pitiful.'

Among tuberculosis patients there were some who insisted that they secreted no phlegm. Mitsu Abé was one of these. Actually they swallowed their phlegm with their saliva, and it had to be removed by means of a rubber tube inserted into the stomach. Three days before Suguro had subjected the woman to this treatment a number of times, and she had finally burst into tears and vomited.

'You couldn't do it, eh?' Toda shrugged his shoulders. 'Well, that's the way it goes. If the Old Man asks, tell him anything at all. Give him your draft number or something.'

The examination rounds began in the wards. Only a faint light lingered at the windows this short February afternoon. When the five of them – the Old Man in his white coat, Dr Asai, Chief Nurse Oba, Toda and Suguro – entered the ward, the nurse in charge hurriedly turned on the lights, which had blackout shades attached; and several flustered patients hastily jumped back into bed and began to arrange themselves properly, hands on knees. The odour which permeated the ward was an uncommon one. Recently many of the patients had been doing their own cooking and so now the smell of firewood mingled with that of the dirty bedding and the urine jars stored beneath the beds to form an amalgamated stink which floated out into the corridor.

Suguro noticed that, depending upon whether he was with the Old Man or alone when he came into the ward, the expressions on the faces of the patients were utterly different. When he came alone, they would smile slyly from their tattered beds, complaining of various grievances and pleading with him: 'Dr Suguro, how about some cough medicine. I can't sleep with this cough.' 'Doctor, could I have some calcium pills?' Suguro knew what they were up to. They secretly hoarded whatever they could get out of him and used it for bartering to supplement the skimpy ration of potatoes and beans that made up their diet. Then there were some who in times of especially severe food shortage took sedatives in order to still the pangs of their empty stomachs.

But when the Old Man came in once a week, flanked by interns and medical students, the patients hastily made themselves as inconspicuous as possible. Asai would hand the temperature chart hanging at the end of the bed to the Old Man; and the patient, his eyes narrowed and filled with distress, would cringe before the great ones as though awaiting a sentence of condemnation. They would try desperately to conceal it if their fevers had gone up or their coughs grown more severe. They would sit, shoulders hunched, hands on knees, hoping to escape the scrutiny of these awesome doctors as quickly as possible.

'Open your pyjamas,' Asai ordered a man. 'Turn over on your stomach. The rash is the same as before, but pus is starting to come out of the ear.'

But the Old Man, holding the temperature chart, seemed to have his mind elsewhere. The ward was dimly lit, and since he had not even bothered to put on his glasses, it was unlikely that he was able to make out the chart.

'Fever?' the Old Man asked dully.

'Since the pain in the ear started, it's gone up above a hundred.'

'It doesn't hurt any more, Doctor.' The middle-aged patient, his bony chest visible through his ragged pyjamas, screwed up his unshaven face in an almost tearful protest. 'It doesn't hurt at all now.'

The symptoms were clear enough. There was a small protuberance by the right ear resulting from swollen lymph glands. Stretching out the hand in which he held his cigarette, the Old Man pressed a long, white finger firmly upon the swelling. The patient cringed, suppressing a cry.

'It's nothing, Doctor.'

39

'So you say, uh?'

'Doctor, I'll be all right, won't I?'

Without a word, the Old Man moved on to the next bed. As Suguro walked behind Toda and Chief Nurse Oba, he heard Asai behind him whispering in a soothing voice as he ran his pen over the temperature chart. 'Don't worry now. We'll give you some pain killer.'

The Old Man was not as testy today as Suguro had expected. Rather than being irascible, he gave the impression of being entirely taken up with something else. As he held a fever chart or rested his hand on a patient's blanket, he seemed not to notice the grey ashes which fell from the cigarette in his finely shaped fingers. He would stand in front of each patient's bed and then, without so much as a gesture, move on to the next. Suguro breathed a sigh of relief. With the Old Man in this mood, there would be no harsh words about the matter of Mitsu Abé's stomach fluid report.

Outside a grey evening mist began to flow in over the hospital grounds. From the kennels some distance away, where the dogs used for experiments were kept, came an insistent hungry barking. Inhibited by their blackout shades, the light bulbs cast a feeble glow only on their immediate surroundings. Suguro looked out at the sea, dark beyond the grey mist. The Medical School was not far from the ocean.

The examinations were over, but still the patients sat up dutifully on their beds and with fearful gaze followed the movements of the doctors. In the uneven light, their elongated shadows ranged grotesquely over the walls behind them. In one corner a woman who was no longer able to hold herself back coughed violently into her hands.

'All right, that's good enough.' In a voice worn with fatigue, the Old Man pushed aside the temperature chart

40

which Asai had offered him. 'No patient in crisis, is there, Asai?'

'You're tired, Sir. Why don't we call it a day?'

Asai, his face puckered with solicitude, smiled a smile of unqualified servility. Toda stood sullenly by, his hands jammed into the pockets of his coat.

'There's just one thing.' Asai turned all at once towards Suguro, speaking very deliberately. 'Suguro here's been checking a patient.'

'Who?'

'The woman welfare case over here.'

As soon as she heard this, the old lady, on her more than ordinarily shabby bed over by the entrance of the ward, started violently and hugged an old army blanket tighter around her body.

'It's all right. Just lie quietly.' As before, Asai gave the patient the benefit of his soothing tones. And as he spoke, with the tip of his shoe, he deftly flicked under her bed the old lady's battered aluminium rice bowl, which had fallen to the floor.

'Actually, he knows himself there's no hope, but Suguro has some idea about an operation.'

'Uh.' The Old Man's tone was listless. He obviously had neither curiosity nor interest to spare.

'It's rather a good opportunity. In the left lung there are two diseased areas, and there's an area of permeation in the right. Therefore the idea would be an experimental operation on both lungs.'

The old lady gazed up, clutching the edge of the blanket to her chest, intimidated by Suguro's tense, strained face. The light did not shine directly on her bed, and she seemed to be taking advantage of the dark shadow to hide herself, hunching her body up as small as possible. She knew that right in front of her these great doctors were talking about

41

her; so she held her breath and kept bobbing her head apologetically.

'Dr Shibata said that he would certainly like to give it a try.'

'Uh.'

'So, I'm having Suguro do a preliminary examination. After that it is for you to decide, Sir.'

Asai glanced back over his shoulder at Suguro. 'That all right?'

Suguro appealed with a glance to Chief Nurse Oba and Toda. But Chief Nurse Oba's expression was as rigid as that of a Noh mask, and Toda, as Toda would, looked away.

'You'll do that, Suguro?' Asai pushed relentlessly.

'Yes.' Blinking, Suguro answered in a thin voice.

After the Old Man had gone out of the ward, Suguro leaned wearily against the wall and let out a deep sigh. The old lady, huddled to one side of the bed and still clutching her blanket, was looking up at him. Distressed, he averted his eyes from that dumb, troubled gaze. In general the chances of the patients in here surviving an operation were no more than fifty-fifty. Furthermore, in the entire history of the Medical School, there had been only two operations successfully performed upon patients who had both lungs infected. In the other ninety-five per cent of such operations, the result had been the death of the patient. But whether there were an operation or not, certainly within half a year her infirmities would prove too much for her and she would die of sheer weakness.

'Today everybody is on the way out. The poor bastard who doesn't die in the hospital gets his chance every night to die in an air raid.' Suguro recalled Toda's bitter comment of shortly before. After the examinations were finished, hollow coughing echoed for a time in the ward.

The patients crawled in and out of their beds like fluttering bats. Suguro felt the oppressive stink of the ward. If human death had a smell attached to it, he thought listlessly, then this was it.

2

No doubt it was a time when everybody was on the way out. If a man didn't breath his last in the hospital, he might well die that night in an air raid. The Medical School and hospital were about five miles out in the country, away from Fukuoka; and so they had not received any direct attacks from the air. Still there was a chance of being hit at any time. The old wings of the hospital, which were made of wood, had been left as they were; but the concrete main building and the research laboratory building had been blackened with tar. If one looked from the roof of the main building upon the city beneath, one could see that day by day Fukuoka was diminishing. Though when one thought about it, it would probably be more accurate to say that every day the brown desert of the burnt-out section was expanding. Whether the day were windy or not, grey ashes swirled up from the brown desert. Some of these small whirlwinds played about the hollowed shell of the Fukiya Department Store, which some years before had made such an overwhelming impression upon the country boy Suguro. Whether there was an air raid alarm or not made little difference. Without let-up, from somewhere in the low, leaden, winter sky would come a dull, rumbling echo and often the sudden staccato sound like beans popping. Last year, when the Chushu section had been hit hard and the Yaku'n area completely razed by fire, there had been panic among the patients and the students. But now hardly anyone asked about whatever section had been burnt most recently. No one any longer paid much attention to whether people lived or died. The medical students were for the most part scattered throughout the city, assigned to aid stations or factories. Suguro too, as an intern, would soon be sent somewhere on his term of temporary service.

To the west of the Medical School, one could see the ocean. Whenever Suguro climbed to the roof, he looked out at the sea. Sometimes its blue brilliance was painfully dazzling. At other times its dark surface was subdued and melancholy. Then he could forget to some extent the War and the hospital and his empty stomach. The changing colours of the sea gave rise to a variety of day-dreams. Once the War was over, he too, like the Old Man, could go to Germany to study and have a love affair with a girl there. And if this were too much, then something ordinary – it didn't matter. To go to a small town somewhere, have a little hospital, marry the daughter of one of the town notables – that would be all right too. If he did that, he would be able to take care of his parents, who lived in Itojima, easily enough. The ordinary, that was the best, Suguro thought.

Unlike Toda, Suguro, even in his college days, had no taste for novels or poems. He remembered only a single poem of those Toda had taught him. One day as he was looking out at the sea in one of its sparkling blue phases, he found, strangely enough, this poem on his lips:

> When the clouds like sheep pass,
> When the clouds swirl like steam,

44

> Sky, your scattering is white,
> White like streams of cotton.

'Sky, your scattering is white, / White like streams of cotton.' Why when Suguro recited that single verse to himself, especially in recent weeks, did he feel himself being overcome by a mood of tears? Ever since he had begun the pre-operation examinations on the old lady, he often came up to the roof and thought about this poem.

Whenever an operation involved cutting through bone, it was essential beforehand to determine the exact physical condition of the patient. Asai had relegated this work to Suguro. Almost every other day, Suguro had to bring the old lady into the examination laboratory and submit her to cardiograph tests, urinalysis, and to have blood taken from her arms, which were reduced to hardly more than skin and bone. Every time he inserted the needle, she would wince with pain. Then, in a corner of the unheated room, she would have to squat with her buttocks pressed to the glass urine container, shivering without let-up.

She did not vomit any blood, but after the examination was over, she began to run a moderate fever, something which had not happened before. Still, perhaps because she wanted so much to be cured, she earnestly complied with everything which Suguro ordered her to do; and when he looked at her, he could not bear to meet her gaze.

'Why did you agree to the operation?'

'What . . . ?' His question had plunged the old lady into forlorn confusion. Why did she agree to the operation? She hadn't the least idea what he meant.

'Why did you say it was all right?'

'Dr Shibata, he said it had to be done. Nothing else to do.'

In the course of a week, bit by bit he gathered and tabu-

45

lated the examination data. Her lungs were functioning better than he had expected, but the number of red corpuscles was decreasing. Also her heart was weak. Suguro realized that the probability of her dying during the operation was about ninety-five per cent.

'Doctor, this operation is going to help me, isn't it?'

When she questioned him like this, there was little he could say to console her. What could he say to her – she who with or without an operation would die within a few months anyway? Suguro had no idea what to tell her. For him the cruel thing was to submit this dying woman to the further pain of an operation. What else was there for Suguro to do but to blink his eyes and keep quiet?

'At any rate, there's the matter of her heart getting weaker.' Suguro made his report to Asai. Asai was having a glass of wine, from the hospital medicinal stock, with Dr Shibata. 'I don't know, but it seems to me that an operation might not be advisable.'

'I know it wouldn't be advisable,' said Dr Shibata, leafing rapidly through the reports which Suguro had brought. One or two glasses of wine had been enough to redden his face considerably. 'No need for you to worry about it, Suguro. After all, I'm going to be the one with the knife, eh? And at any rate, she's a welfare patient isn't she?'

'Suguro's concerned, Doctor, because he's in charge of her,' Asai interjected with a smile, his tone at its sweetest pitch. 'I used to be the same way myself.'

'Well, I'm going to give something a try with our welfare patient.' Staggering just a bit, Dr Shibata went over to the blackboard and took a piece of chalk out of the pocket of his white coat. 'It's not going to be the usual Schmidt technique, not at all. Suguro, did you read Corio's thesis?'

'Whose?'

46

'About his transformation method. Well, pay attention. Below the upper rib section, spread and make an incision. Then you cut the ribs beginning with the fourth, then the second, the third, and the first. This is Corio's method. I'm going to pay close attention to the shape of the diseased area and the direction of the bronchial tubes.'

Suguro bowed and left the room. Out in the corridor, he pressed his face for a time against a window. For he felt unusually fatigued. A feeling of heaviness oppressed him. The old odd job man who worked for the hospital was out digging up the ground, wearing his boots. Above him the tips of poplar branches covered with swelling buds swayed in the wind. He turned up the black earth with his shovel, throwing it to one side, repeating the monotonous action time after time. A truck drove up raising dust and passed in front of the laboratory building. On top of the truck huddled a number of tall men of dishevelled appearance, wearing green fatigue uniforms. After it had stopped at the entrance of Second Surgery, two soldiers with pistols slung at their hips opened the door of the truck and energetically leaped down. In contrast to the vigorous movement of the soldiers, the group wearing the fatigue uniforms dragged their feet and moved lackadaisically as they climbed the steps to the entrance. Since they towered over their guards, even Suguro was able to tell at a glance that they were American prisoners.

'There're some American prisoners over in Second Surgery,' Suguro informed Toda when he came back to Laboratory Number Three. 'A truck brought them.'

Toda was scratching around inside a drawer of his desk.

'So, what's so strange about that? They brought some before for typhus shots, didn't they?' Not finding what he wanted, Toda slammed the drawer irritably. 'Now where

47

the devil did my stethoscope go to? Hey, Suguro, let me take yours for a minute.'

'What for?'

'There's one more patient who's going to be operated on. Dr Asai and I are in charge of the examination. Don't get excited. It's not the old lady.' The withering smile of condescension with which Toda always imparted wisdom to Suguro was a trait dating back to college days. He spoke in a hushed tone. 'Who do you think it is, Suguro?'

'I haven't the least idea.'

'Mrs Tabé, in the private room. She's a relative of the late Dean, the nurses say. That lady is the one.'

Even without Toda's information, Suguro knew about the young and beautiful patient named Tabé. Usually the general examinations began in the wards, continued in the second floor second-class rooms, and finished in the private rooms. Once in the private rooms, even the Old Man's manner of speaking and his examination procedure became polite, especially so with regard to this pretty young married woman. With her he displayed the greatest deference. Suguro and the nurses could see written on the top of the temperature chart 'A relative of Dean Osugi' in Asai's hand.

He could see from her case history that she was very young. There was a moderate cavity in the upper section of her right lung and a number of small infected areas. But since the pleura itself was infected, pneumothorax treatment could not be given. She lay resignedly upon her bed, always face up, her long black hair spread out upon the immaculate pillow case. Apparently she was fond of reading, for a number of books unfamiliar to Suguro lined the shelf beneath the large window which caught the sun most of the day. When her breasts were exposed during the examination, her skin did not seem to be that of a sick

48

woman, so lovely was it. Her husband was a naval officer, they said, stationed somewhere far off. Perhaps because of that, the tips of her full breasts were small and red like those of a young girl. Once a day a woman who was most likely her mother came with a maid who carried a basket containing her meals. It was, all in all, a world quite different from that of the ward patients.

'You're on the way to recovery, Mrs Tabé.' When he put aside his stethoscope, the Old Man exuded well being. 'I'll soon be able to demonstrate that to you. But it's little enough for me to do, considering all that I owe to the kindness of Doctor Osugi.'

Still, an operation was necessary, and the time set for it had been the coming autumn. Why, Suguro wondered, was it suddenly moved forward to February? Had the Old Man noticed something during the previous examination? If he had, he had not mentioned it.

'Why was it moved forward all at once?'

'That's the problem, isn't it? The Old Man hasn't been putting much into the examinations recently. So this operation. . . .' Toda craned his neck and looked out of the window from his chair. In front of the entrance to Second Surgery, the two soldiers, their hands clenched behind their backs, paced like animals in a cage. Under the poplar tree, the old man with the boots went on moving his shovel as before.

'I have an idea that this operation has something to do with the Old Man's getting the dean's chair.'

He sat down again and, tearing a page from a small Japanese-German dictionary, scooped some of his tobacco ration from a can on the desk.

'What the Old Man can do is this. He'll gain quite a lot of credit from a successful operation on this woman. The election for the dean will be in April. The patient's a relative of the Osugis. The disease is limited to the upper section of one lung. She's not at all debilitated. Instead of waiting until the autumn, do it this month, so by April the stage will be well set. Then all the doctors from Internal Medicine belonging to the Osugi faction will be inclined in favour of the Old Man. In this way Doctor Kando of Second can be overpowered before the election.'

Pronouncing his words strongly and deliberately, Toda exhaled his cigarette-smoke in a way which was characteristic of him. Toda, who was from a wealthy Osaka family, had from college on been wont to explain to the country-bred Suguro the intricacies of human relations in the Medical School and the devious undertakings of the hospital factions against a backdrop of cigarette smoke.

'Sweetness and sentimentality are forbidden luxuries for a doctor.' The sadder the expression in Suguro's blinking eyes, the more gleeful Toda's. 'Doctors aren't saints. They want to be successful. They want to become full professors. And when they want to try out new techniques, they don't limit their experiments to monkeys and dogs. Suguro, this is the world, and you ought to take a closer look at it.'

'So you were told to make the examination then?' Suguro asked. He sat down in a chair and closed his eyes. The weariness he had felt just before in the corridor came rushing back upon him. 'I don't know. I just don't know.'

'What's the trouble?'

'The old lady's going into Dr Shibata's experimental lab, and Mrs Tabé is going to be a means towards the Old Man's advancement.'

'Of course? What do you want? What's wrong with that? First of all, why are you so taken with the old lady to the exclusion of everything else?' Toda grinned, looking at Suguro's distraught face. 'Yes, what's so bad about it?'

'I don't know how to put it, but. . . .'

50

'Oh come off it! Killing a patient isn't so solemn a matter as all that. It's nothing new in the world of medicine. That's how we've made our progress! Right now in the city all kinds of people are dying all the time in the air raids, and nobody thinks twice about it. Rather than have the old lady die in an air raid, why not kill her here at the hospital. There'd be some meaning in that, boy!'

'What kind of meaning?' Suguro muttered in a hollow voice.

'Why it's obvious! If she died in an air raid, the most that she could hope for would be that her bones were thrown into the Naka River. But if she gets killed during an operation, no doubt about it, she becomes a living pillar upholding the temple of medical science. And won't the old lady, looking ahead to the day when numberless TB victims are brought back to health along the road she has helped to open up, more fittingly be able to close her eyes in peace?'

'You're really a tough customer.' Suguro heaved a deep sigh. 'I can get the picture too. Yes. Yes. . . .'

'How can you live if you're not tough?' Abruptly Toda let out a twisted, mocking laugh. 'You're a real ass, you know! Today, is there any other way to get by?'

'If there were, would you take it?'

'Good question. But right now, quick, how about that stethoscope?'

'It's . . . it's in my instrument case.'

Suguro left the room. As he stood in the garden, the wind blew in his face, and he listlessly watched the old man in the boots moving his shovel.

'Digging a slit trench?'

'No. Have to take down the poplar. The thing's grown so nice too. But the college people say cut it down. Don't ask me why.'

51

In front of Second Surgery, the two soldiers with hands clenched behind their backs had disappeared. The truck, too, which had brought the prisoners was gone. Suguro climbed the stairs to the roof of the main building, which had lapsed into silence again, his shoes echoing noisily on the stairs. Below him was spread the wide campus of the Medical School. To the right were a wing for contagious diseases and a building containing the classrooms for First Internal Medicine. The medical research building and the library, both blackened with tar, together with a wooden hospital wing, which lay between them, formed three more ranks. Grey smoke climbed from the stack of the sterilization unit. There were about one hundred patients. About how many nurses and other employees were there, he wondered. He had the feeling that he was a cog on one of the gear wheels turning here, whose movements he had no way of understanding. 'There's no figuring it out,' he muttered to himself. 'It doesn't pay to think about it.'

The sea today looked dark and threatening. Brown dust swirled up from Fukuoka and seemed to soil the clouds, which were the colour of old cotton wool, and even the pale sun. Win the War, lose the War – it was all the same to Suguro. The effort it cost even to think about such things weighed oppressively upon him.

3

'Fifty six aeons, seven thousand eras is the age of Bodhi-
sattva Nikin. To those who are true of heart, a light will
surely be revealed. . . .'

'Just like that is all right. Lie still now.'

'Yes, Doctor.'

While Suguro was making his examination, the old lady
kept her eyes shut and listened to the prayer chanted by
Mitsu Abé, who was in the bed next to her. Mitsu wasn't a
welfare patient; but since they were about the same age
and their beds were next to each other, they would frequently talk to each other in low voices.

'That's a poem isn't it?'

'Oh, you! No, it's a prayer by Shinran,' Mitsu Abé said
wagging her chin towards the old lady. 'Doctor, would it
be all right if I read her something from this holy book
about Buddha? She asked me to.'

'Go ahead.'

Mitsu took her glasses from her bag, adjusted them on
her nose and sat up straight on the bed. She took a small
book with dog-eared pages and, reverently elevating it to
the level of her eyes, began to read:

' "The Lord Buddha deigned one day . . . to visit one of
his disciples who was sick. The disciple was suffering
grievously because he was unable to pass his urine or faeces.
The Lord Buddha. . . ." Doctor, what's this word?'

' "Hospitably." Isn't this a children's book?'

'Yes, Doctor. The lady in that bed over there let me take
it. ". . . hospitably visited him. 'Did you,' he asked, 'when
you were in good health, watch beside the beds of your
friends who were sick? Know that you are suffering so
terribly all by yourself because you failed to care for others
before. And now do you feel how sharp the pain is? When

you cross to the other world, you will be tortured with pains that your heart will not be able to bear.' " '

While Mitsu read on in a stumbling voice, the old lady kept her eyes shut. Her aluminium dish, with some brown potato skins left in it, fell from the bed on to the floor. The patients around became silent and pricked up their ears.

'Then what happens is that Lord Buddha cures him and makes him so that he's not mean and selfish any more.'

Like a child, the old lady bobbed her head again and again on hearing her friend's confident exegesis. Suguro put away his stethoscope. How would he go about breaking the thing to her, he wondered.

'You ought to tell him.' Mitsu turned to Suguro to explain. 'She feels down at the mouth about her operation. She would've liked to see her boy first and be easy in her mind when she had the operation.'

'She has children?'

'Yes, Doctor. Her boy is in the Army somewhere.'

Mitsu Abé scrambled down from the bed and rummaged in a wicker basket beneath it and brought out a carefully folded Rising Sun flag. The dyed emblem, looking as though it would run in the first rain, showed reddish-yellow against the cheap white cloth of the field.

'We're getting everybody here in the ward to write something on it for her boy. So, Doctor, would you please write something too?'

'All right.'

Suguro took the flag in his hands, and as he did, he knew he could not tell the old lady that the day was set for the operation. It had been announced that morning. First, next Friday morning, would be Mrs Tabé's operation, performed by the Old Man. Then one week later, Dr Shibata would perform the operation on the old lady. Toda and Suguro were assigned to assist at both. He brooded over the pain the scalpel would inflict, the dull sound of snapping rib bones. With the other patients it was bad enough to have to make the announcement which brought a week of distress; but at the prospect of telling it to this woman who was almost sure to die, his courage left him completely.

When he returned to the chilly laboratory, he pushed aside some test tubes and a pair of tongs, and he spread out on the desk the Rising Sun flag which Mitsu Abé had given him. What could he write? He hadn't the faintest idea of what to write. Scrawled on the cheap white fabric were the messages written by the ward patients. When this flag finally reached the son, whom the ward patients praised as 'pure' and 'gallant', his mother would probably be no more than a corpse. That image floated vacantly in his mind. He took one of Toda's cigarettes from the desk drawer and lit it. After a period of fruitless thought, he finally, with a sinking heart, put down some sort of hackneyed sentiment about the necessity of victory.

As if to confirm all that Toda had conjectured, the preparations for Mrs Tabé's operation were carried out with the most scrupulous care and solicitude. Toda was as Toda always was, but Asai, who realized that the success or failure of this operation was of vital concern to First Surgery to which he had immediately linked his own fortunes, went about his duties with the utmost earnestness. Asai looked forward with trepidation to the next day, next year and thereafter, when the young doctors who had been his colleagues, their tours of duty over, would return to the hospital and the laboratories. Until then he had by all means to establish firmly a relationship in which the Old Man relied on him completely. So he was determined not to miss a single chance to advance himself in the Medical School, through the benevolent patronage of its most distinguished surgeon. However, Dr Shibata – this too was Toda's analysis – was apparently jealous of the Old Man's pre-eminence. For Shibata had not been trained under the Old Man but was a protégé of the previous chief surgeon of First, Dr Shimogaki.

The examinations of the doctor in charge were as a rule limited to two a week; but, before this particular operation, the Old Man examined Mrs Tabé almost every day.

'By autumn, you'll be home, Dr Asai assured her as he held up in front of the window the chest X-ray photos which he had brought to show her. 'After that it would be best to rest in the country for a few months, and the following year you'll be completely recovered.'

Perhaps because the prospect of winning the dean's chair in April buoyed him with a surging expectancy, the Old Man seemed to have regained his old self-confidence. Puffing a cigarette, both hands thrust in the pockets of his spotless white coat, he strode the hospital corridors resolutely. The slightly stooped, withdrawn, meditative figure fulfilled perfectly for the unsophisticated Suguro the image which the title *Doctor* evoked in him. And as he dragged his military shoes behind Toda and Chief Nurse Oba, he felt once again the yearning sense of reverence that he used to have towards the Old Man.

'Doctor, is everything all right about my daughter's operation?'

Recently Mrs Tabé's refined mother had been in her room almost constantly. She wore black *monpe*, the trousers that had become equivalent to a uniform for women during the War. The young wife smiled from her bed. She was sitting up. While fingering the neck of her nightgown with one hand, with the other she brushed back the hair which hung down over her cheek.

'It's all a matter of routine,' said the Old Man. 'In an operation everything is done while the patient is sleeping under anaesthetic. Naturally the night after there'll be a certain amount of discomfort. She'll feel rather thirsty perhaps. So then, it will be a matter of being patient for two or three days.'

'But as for any danger . . . ?' The mother frowned slightly as she spoke.

At her words Asai laughed on cue in his soothing feminine tones. 'Ah, Mrs Masuda, what an opinion you must have of Dr Hashimoto's skill and all our efforts.'

In reassuring her, Asai, for once, was not straying too far from the truth. Mrs Tabé was in the best possible condition for an operation as regards blood count, heart condition etc. Suguro, who had not yet performed an operation, felt that even he could have carried out this one successfully.

As he watched the Old Man, his stethoscope pressed to the girl's full breast, listening to her heartbeat, he wondered of what his feeling of jealously was compounded. Was he jealous of the girl's husband, jealous of a happiness which Suguro himself would never be able to gain? Or was it rather that he simply felt a sort of just anger on behalf of all those patients who lay in the dark ward? Whatever it was he felt, he couldn't explain it to himself.

It was Thursday night. The night before the operation it was the job of the nurses to shave the body hair off the patient and rub her with alcohol. Toda, Suguro, and Chief Nurse Oba were in the laboratory until very late selecting and arranging the photos which would be needed in the course of the operation. At last Suguro was ready to leave for the ten minute walk which would take him to his boarding house. As he stepped outside, he heard in the distance the sound of a car engine approaching in the darkness of the grounds.

When the car passed in front of him, he caught a brief glimpse of Dr Kando's face illumined fleetingly by the dashboard light, beside him a stocky little officer who sat with clenched jaw, both hands on his sword hilt. Suguro felt that Dr Kando's face had a somehow unclean look about it. He felt himself touched by a dark shadow.

'I hope the Old Man wins!' he told himself. Tomorrow would be a crucial day in the behind the scenes struggle between these doctors, a struggle in which he had wanted no part. But now, for the first time, he felt excitement.

It was ten o'clock on Friday morning. Asai, Toda, and Suguro waited outside the operating theatre for the patient to be brought up. They wore white surgical gowns over rubber aprons and had sandals on their feet.

The sky was overcast. The operating theatre was off to one side of the second floor of the hospital, and so no nurses or convalescent patients were liable to intrude here. The sun shone dully on the floor of the long empty corridor.

After a while those waiting heard the distant squeak of wheels. Then they saw the trolley carrying Mrs Tabé slowly approaching, pushed by a nurse and her mother. Because of the preliminary anaesthetic injection received in her room and because of her fear of what was to come, the woman's face was drained of blood as she lay on the trolley, and her hair was in disorder.

'Be brave now!' As the trolley began gradually to move more quickly, her mother hurried a little to keep up with it.

58

'Mother's here with you. And your sister will soon be here too. The operation will be over before you know it.'

The weary girl opened her eyes, as frantic as those of a snared bird, and tried to whisper something; but her voice would not come.

'The Doctor will take care of everything,' her mother cried to her again. 'The Doctor will!'

Standing behind the Old Man, who had already washed his hands in alcohol, Chief Nurse Oba fastened the strings of his surgical gown. Then like a mother taking care of a son taller than herself, she put on him the white surgical cap, which resembled a fez. Another nurse held out a metal box containing the rubber surgical gloves. And with that the Old Man, his face like a Noh mask, took on an uncanny appearance, like some pure white totemic image.

Throughout the operation it was necessary to maintain a temperature of seventy degrees in the operating theatre, and already it was warm and stuffy. In order to wash away dust and the inevitable blood, water streamed over the floor in a light trickle. It reflected the light from the huge ceiling lamp, and the entire operating theatre shone with a glow like burnished platinum. Immersed in this glow, Asai and the nurses moved about, their figures wavering in it like seaweed swayed by ocean currents. Toda tested the instrument for cutting the patient's shoulder blade.

The two nurses placed the now naked Mrs Tabé on the operating table, on her side with her legs drawn up. The Old Man with a practised hand began to take the instruments from the metal box which stood on the glass stand beside the operating table and to arrange them. The scalpel for displacing the pleura, the instrument for cutting the rib bones, the clamps, and the others – they clattered slightly as they struck one against another. When Mrs Tabé heard this faint sound, her body trembled for an instant; but then, as though heavily fatigued, she shut her eyes once more.

'It won't hurt at all, Mrs Tabé,' said Asai in a mellow tone. 'We'll soon have you under anaesthetic.'

'Is everything ready?' The Old Man's voice was low but it echoed from the walls of the room.

'Yes, Doctor,' Asai replied.

'All right, let's begin.'

Everyone turned in unison towards the Old Man and the patient and bowed silently. The silence spread through the theatre. Then Chief Nurse Oba moved, beginning to wipe the patient's white back with cotton soaked in tincture of iodine.

'Scalpel.'

The Old Man took the electric scalpel held out to him in the powerful grip of his right hand and bent slightly forward. A sizzling noise struck Suguro's ears. It was the sound of muscles being severed and burnt by electricity. One instant the smooth white curve of flesh held the eye, and in the next all was wiped out by the image of dark, oozing blood. Asai deftly stopped the flow from the severed blood vessels, and then Suguro sutured them one by one with silk thread.

'Pleura displacer,' the Old Man ordered. 'Blood intake?'

The transfusion needle had been thrust into Mrs Tabé's white leg. Before answering Suguro checked the flow of the rubber tube from the container holding the liqiud compound of stimulants, vitamins, dextrose, and adrenaline into the patient's body.

'Normal.'

'Blood pressure?'

'All right,' the nurse replied.

A long time passed. Suddenly Mrs Tabé began to moan. Besides the regular anaesthetic, procaine had been given her, but still she seemed to be half conscious.

'It hurts, Mother. I can't breathe. . . .'

Sweat began to flow over the Old Man's forehead. Chief Nurse Oba wiped it with a piece of gauze.

'I can't breathe, Mother. I can't breathe.'

'Raspatory!'

When the pleura had been cut aside, the white rib bones became visible. The Old Man began to cut these resolutely with an instrument resembling a pair of secateurs. From beneath his mask a suppressed grunt could be heard as he put his strength into what he was doing. With a dull snapping noise, the fourth rib, which resembled the antler of a deer, was wrenched off and dropped into a receptacle with a dry echo. The network of flesh covering the chest wall and inner chest surged up like a red balloon from the pressure of the lung beneath. The sound of the Old Man's low grunts, the snapping of the rib bones, and the dry sound of their dropping into the receptacle echoed through the operating theatre. Sweat once more covered the forehead of the Old Man, and the chief nurse stretched up again and again to wipe it away.

'Blood intake?'

'Normal.'

'Pulse? Blood pressure?'

'All right.'

'I'm taking the first rib.'

Now the most critical point in this kind of operation had come.

Suguro noticed that Mrs Tabé's blood had suddenly darkened. Instantly a chill premonition struck him. But the Old Man went on silently cutting the muscles about the rib. Nor did the nurse say anything after checking the blood pressure gauge. Asai, too, was silent.

'Excision scalpel,' the Old Man ordered, and he seemed

61

all at once to tremble slightly. 'Is the irrigator all right?' He had noticed the darkening blood, a clear indication that something was wrong.

Suguro saw that his sweaty face shone as though glazed with wax.

'Any abnormality?'

'The blood pressure is. . . .' The voice of the young nurse suddenly rose in panic. 'The blood pressure is down.'

'Apply the oxygen inhaler,' Asai ordered frantically. 'Hurry!'

'There's sweat in my eyes! Sweat in my eyes!' The Old Man staggered as he spoke. The chief nurse's hand trembled as she wiped his forehead.

'Quick with the gauze.'

They applied gauze, trying to staunch the flow of blood, but with no success. The Old Man worked his hands frantically.

'Gauze! Gauze! Blood pressure?'

'Way down.'

At that moment the Old Man turned his face Suguro's way. It was twisted with distress, the face of a child about to burst into tears.

'Blood pressure?'

'None at all,' Asai answered. He had already taken off his mask, and he threw it down upon the floor.

'She's dead.' The nurse who checked the woman's pulse murmured in a crushed voice.

When the nurse dropped the dead woman's hand, the arm of the corpse, which was torn and blood-splattered like a ripped pomegranate, flopped limply back upon the edge of the operating table. The Old Man stood as though in a stupor. No one said a word. The water kept flowing over the floor, reflecting the brightness pouring down from the ceiling lamp.

'Doctor,' whispered Asai. 'Doctor.'

The Old Man turned towards him, but his stare was vacant.

'We'll have to put things in order.'

'Put things in order . . . ? Yes . . . yes, of course.'

'What's the best way? Anyway, I'll close the incisions.'

Mrs Tabé's sunken eyes were rigidly opened, and, with her red tongue protruding slightly, her mouth was wide open in a fool's gape. She seemed to be staring fixedly at all of them. Suguro could easily read in the wide staring eyes the proof of the suffering she had endured during the operation. Her stomach, hands, and face were smeared with blood.

Suguro squatted down on the floor, the strength utterly gone from his legs. Somewhere inside his head, he heard incessantly a faint sound like that of glass shattering. He felt nausea overcoming him. He rubbed his eyes repeatedly with his hand and wiped the sweat from his forehead.

Taking over for the Old Man, Asai quickly sewed up the woman's body as though she had been a torn quilt, and the nurses began to wipe it with alcohol.

'Put on bandages,' Asai ordered sharply. 'Wrap it thoroughly in bandages.'

The Old Man slumped down on a chair and kept staring listlessly at a spot on the floor. He paid not the least attention to the sounds in the room or the voices of the interns.

'Take the patient back to her room. Not one word now to the family about the operation.'

As Asai said this in a tense, strained voice, he looked at each of them. His words sent a chill through them, and they shrank back instinctively towards the wall.

'As soon as we get back to the patient's room, give her

63

an injection of Ringer's solution. And do everything else besides, just as you would after any operation. The patient is not dead. She will die tomorrow morning.'

Asai's voice was not the usual sweet, high-pitched voice heard in the laboratory. His rimless glasses had slid down on his nose, which was slippery with sweat.

The young nurse walked somewhat unsteadily as she pushed the trolley on which the sheet-covered body lay. She seemed unequal to the effort this required. In the corridor the dead woman's mother and a girl who was apparently her sister hurried over when they caught a glimpse of the pale face on the trolley.

'She came through the operation in excellent shape.'

Making a great effort, Asai showed every sign of composure and smiled a smile which must have cost him dearly, but he was unable to do anything about the hoarseness of his voice. Chief Nurse Oba placed herself between the mother and sister and the trolley, blocking them as effectively as she could.

'But tonight will be a difficult one of course. Just to be on the safe side, we've got to forbid visitors for a day or two.'

'Does that include us?' cried the sister in distress.

'I'm sorry but it does. But don't worry. Chief Nurse Oba and I will spend the night by her bed.'

The door of the patient's room stood open. The young nurse who had been in charge of the blood pressure gauge hurried in, on the verge of tears. She apparently had no idea of the meaning of the orders which Asai had given. Chief Nurse Oba stood by the door holding the box containing the injections. Only this woman with the habitual Noh mask face registered no emotion. From long experience she was the only one who knew exactly what to do in a

64

situation like this. Asai was already waiting inside the room.

Suguro stood sluggishly in the corridor, his face to a window.

'Suguro, keep a lookout here and make sure everything stays hushed up,' Asai had ordered him. From around the corner of the corridor, he heard Toda's voice. Apparently he had stopped Mrs Tabé's mother and sister, who had been coming this way.

'But, please. . . .'

'I'm sorry, Ma'am.'

He heard their voices echoing.

'How did it go?'

Suguro looked up to find Dr Shibata, wearing a surgical gown, studying his face closely.

'Was the operation a success?'

When Suguro had shaken his head, the traces of a sardonic smile instantly began to form on Shibata's sunken-cheeked face.

'Died, huh? Well, that's the way it goes. When was it?'

'The first rib.'

'So? Well, looks like the Old Man, too, is getting on.'

Suguro entered the room. He was at a loss to know what to do. At Asai's order he removed the hypodermic needle for the Ringer solution which was plunged into the leg of the dead woman. He seemed to hear a sound like a clock ticking inside his head, the same sound over and over again: 'What's the use? What's the use? What's the use?'

Toda came in. He offered Suguro one of his hand-rolled cigarettes from a celluloid case. Waving his hand weakly, Suguro refused.

'Our little comedy's moving along nicely.' Glancing about the room, Toda raised the cigarette to his lips. His hand trembled. 'A comedy all right. A real comedy.'

'Comedy?'

'Sure. If she died during the operation, it would have been the Old Man's responsibility completely. But if she died afterwards, maybe it's not the fault of the man with the knife. There's an element of doubt. You can make out a case for the Old Man at election time. Asai has it all worked out.'

Suguro turned round and walked out into the corridor.

'I hope everything is all right.'

Suguro heard the voices of the mother and sister from somewhere down the gloomy, shadowed corridor. He went silently down the stairs. Outside, as darkness began to settle over the campus, a car carrying some nurses passed.

'Miss Sakata!' someone who was perhaps a friend of one of them called out from one of the windows. Greyish smoke flowed up into the sky from the stack of the sterilization unit. Underneath the poplar tree, the old man was still at it with his shovel. It was the usual sunset scene on the campus, the same as every other day.

All at once Suguro felt like laughing, though he didn't know what it was that struck him as so funny.

4

Despite the silence of those involved, the failure of the operation spread through the classrooms and the hospital wings like sewage seeping into the ground. In the nurses' rooms, in the laboratories, whenever there were two or three together, there was no other topic but this rumour. Out of deference to the position of the Tabé family as relatives of

Dean Osugi, there were no public remonstrations; but the doctors on the faculty of Internal Medicine, all of them disciples of the late dean, criticized First Surgery's high-handed method of disregarding the opinion of Internal Medicine and hurrying the operation. At any rate all hope of their recommending the Old Man for election as dean seemed to have died.

All of this now seemed to Suguro a matter of no special moment. It was all the same to him. His mind was a blank and his body sluggish and heavy. He had no interest nor enthusiasm now for his work, for the patients in their beds, for the hospital in general.

Dr Shibata announced in an offhand way, two or three days after Mrs Tabé's death, that the operation on the old lady would be postponed for two or three months.

'If we make it two deaths in a row, the reputation of First Surgery would really be shot to pieces completely, eh?' The doctor's sunken cheeks twisted in a laugh.

Suguro heard all this as though it had to do with events on another planet. He did not feel any happiness at the prospect of being able to let the old lady know.

He watched the old man working with his shovel in the pale winter sunlight of the campus. What is he doing, this old man, Suguro thought, but repeating the same action again and again? Come to think of it, he had been digging in that same spot for over two weeks now. Perhaps the old man was working out a sombre revenge upon those who had ordered the poplar tree to be cut down and upon the era itself, by digging, refilling, digging, refilling.

'Well, what now?' Suguro from time to time would ask himself. 'Is this what it means to be a doctor? Is this a medical school?'

But then, at such times, his thoughts inevitably turned sluggish, and he became muddled. Any day now he would

67

be called up for his term of service. So whatever happened here from now on, it was all the same to him. And this was the mood which settled upon him. But occasionally in the midst of this white blank of frustration, a black anger suddenly surged up in him. It was this emotion that overcame him the day that he slapped the old lady.

One day during his rounds, he secretly left a lump of dextrose beside the old lady's pillow. Mitsu Abé caught him in the act with a sidelong glance but he pretended not to notice. It was not the first time Suguro had done this sort of thing for his welfare patient. The next day when he happened to stop by the ward, the old lady was sleeping with her thin hands over her face. She had not picked up the yellow lump of dextrose he had given her. It was lying on the floor by her bed.

'Like a spoiled child! She depends on me, then she doesn't even take what I give her.' He knew that the old lady could use the dextrose as a valuable barter item in getting food from the other patients, and he felt unaccountably angry.

That afternoon there was a blood pressure check for the ward patients. Mitsu Abé appeared at the laboratory, but the old lady did not.

'Where is she?'

'That one, she said she didn't feel good.'

Suguro went into the deserted ward. The old lady, all by herself, sat huddled on top of her disarranged bed. She had her back to Suguro, and like a rat she was gnawing the lump of dextrose, which she clutched in her two hands. Seeing her wretched figure and yellowed hair, Suguro was overcome by a feeling of unutterable disgust.

'Why didn't you come?'

'Oh!' The old lady, her hands pressed to her mouth, could not answer.

His mind in turmoil, Suguro roughly pulled away her hands, and the old lady fell back upon the dirty spread. He struck the trembling face with his open palm.

The Old Man hardly ever appeared in the laboratory now. In his place Dr Shibata made the bi-weekly ward rounds. In the room where Mrs Tabé had lain, the mattress had been taken from the bed and thrown on the floor and scattered over it were three or four pieces of newspaper with muddy boot prints on them.

The concensus was that because the operation had been a failure, the Old Man did not want to show his face. And so the laboratories, the nurses' room, the hospital wing in general – all took on a slovenly neglected appearance. Grey dust came in through the broken window and settled in the corridor. The nurses on duty neglected their jobs, and the patients themselves disregarded the restrictions of the after lunch quiet period.

'Japan and First Surgery are both in about the same run down condition.' Toda's tone was more than usually scornful as he walked up and down in the unheated room. 'So be it! You'll be off as a medical cadet soon and be done with this place.'

'So be it, huh?' Suguro blinked. 'Me, I don't care what happens. But you, why haven't you asked to be called up?'

If an intern requested immediate service, he could become a medical officer after only a brief period of training.

'Who, me?' Toda's grin as usual was tinged with ridicule. 'To hell with that.'

'If you don't do it, you'll be a private.'

'I'll see what comes. Dying a private's as good as any other way.'

'Why?'

'It all comes out the same no matter what you do. Today everybody's on the way out.'

Later the same day, Suguro saw another truck-load of American prisoners in front of the entrance of Second Surgery. As before two young soldiers stood by the door of the truck with pistols at their hips. As Suguro passed by, the prisoners, gnawing at potatoes they held in their hands, were climbing into the truck. They seemed all the taller and their arms and legs all the longer in their loose baggy fatigue uniforms. One of them held a switch of pine. As he walked by them, neither interest nor curiosity stirred in him. Some of them, with brown beards sprouting on their chins, seemed no more than teenagers. Suguro felt neither pity and sympathy nor hostility and hatred towards these men. He passed them on the path with the lack of concern he felt towards men whom he expected never to see again in his life and whom he would soon forget. But how did they appear to themselves? Surely as something other than mere prisoners. Suguro's mental sluggishness proved a thorough block to further speculation of this sort.

A week after he had seen the prisoners, there was, for the first time in some weeks, a major air raid on Fukuoka. It began in the early afternoon. Since the number of planes was larger than usual, the patients who were able to walk took refuge in the cellar, and the others were carried there on stretchers. Although the Medical School was some distance from the city, the shock of the bombs was enough to shake the windows of the hospital. The exploding anti-aircraft shells kept up a constant chatter, and in the lead coloured sky the lazy drone of the B-29s went on interminably.

Finally, at sunset, the last enemy planes turned back towards their South Sea bases. When Suguro climbed up to the roof, he saw the entire city engulfed in white smoke, which was swirling up from it. The Fukuya Department Store was burning. Whenever the smoke thinned, Suguro could see orange flames flaring up. Then in the east, as though drawn by the flames and smoke, a large black cloud came over the horizon and gradually began to cover the city. All through the night, a cold rain fell, mixed with ashes. At the hospital some hard biscuits obtained from the Army were distributed, five each, as a special ration to all the patients, including those in the wards. Suguro was on watch that night and so did not return to his boarding house. He wrapped his gaiter-clad legs in a blanket and lay down to sleep on a desk in the laboratory.

Sometime before dawn, he was awakened by a nurse. The old lady was dying she said. He ran down to the ward. Mitsu Abé stood all by herself in the faint light of the single candle burning beside the old lady's bed. Was it that none of the other patients knew, or was it that they knew and did not care, their faces buried in their quilts? He shone his flashlight in her face just in time to see it fall to one side as the life went out of her. Saliva flowed from her open mouth. He saw that her left hand was tightly clenched, and he forced it open. One of last night's biscuits, hard as a stone, fell out and rolled upon the floor. When Suguro saw this, he remembered with pain the scene of not long before, the old woman in the deserted ward gnawing at the lump of dextrose with her front teeth. He remembered how he had slapped her face.

'Her boy will get that flag at least,' Mitsu Abé whispered forlornly.

The premonition he had felt when he wrote the cliché about certain victory on the flag had been confirmed. Yet he had been thinking of death in the course of an operation, not a natural death like this. The shock of the raid and the night of cold rain had been too much for her.

The rain continued the next day too. Perhaps because he might have caught a cold, Suguro had a severe headache. The job of disposing of the old woman's body fell to the old odd job man who had been digging beneath the poplar tree. From a window in the laboratory, Suguro watched him and another workman carrying out the wooden crate which contained the body.

'I wonder where they're going to bury her?'

'Don't ask me,' Toda spoke from behind him. 'So with that, your illusion passes. Every attachment is an illusion.'

He *had* been attached to that old woman, and for such a long time. Why? Suguro wondered. Now for the first time, he felt as though he was beginning to understand. 'She was the one thing in the midst of Toda's pessimistic "everybody's on the way out" that I was going to make sure didn't die. She was my first patient. Now there she goes, soaked with the rain, packed into an old orange crate. From now on,' Suguro thought, 'for myself, for the War, for Japan, for everything, let things go just as they like.'

5

After the death of the old woman, Suguro realized that he had caught a cold, probably brought on by the night he spent sleeping in the laboratory. He had a fever and felt enervated. As he sat working at his desk beside Toda, his head throbbed, and he seemed on the verge of vomiting.

'Was the old lady's TB catching? Your face, anyhow, is way off colour, sort of on the grey side,' said Toda.

Suguro took a look for himself. He saw that his face was indeed grey and puffy, his eyes dull and glazed.

'Dr Shibata wants to see both of you.' A nurse put her head in at the door. She was the one who had been in charge of the blood pressure gauge on the day of the operation.

'What? Does he want us now?'

'Yes, he said right away.'

'I've got an awful headache.'

Bearing up as well as he could with his nausea, Suguro went with Toda to Number Two Laboratory. When they entered Shibata and Asai, in company with a plump, red-faced medical officer, were seated comfortably. The officer cast a flickering glance at the two interns.

'O.K.' And with that single word, he got up and left.

In the charcoal brazier blue fumes blazed from the silver embers. On top of the table were packets of cigarettes and some tea cups which had been filled with wine.

'Sit down. There. Our medical officer has left us, but not without leaving us some of his bounty.'

Shibata, squeaking his swivel chair, swung his legs loosely back and forth for a while.

'Go ahead and smoke, Suguro, Toda. Avail yourselves of the military's bounty.'

Asai got up and turning his back went over to the window to look out. Both Suguro and Toda knew that there was something on their minds, and that they had deliberately planned this session.

'Toda, your research topic is the cavity induction treatment, isn't it?' A made-to-measure smile lit the hollow-cheeked face. 'How are you doing with it? Nowadays it's pretty hard to get anything done. Aside from Monaldi's

73

theory, it's impossible to get your hands on any new documents, eh?'

Without answering, Toda took a cigarette from the 'bounty' and lit it. Now the distinctive odour of tobacco and burning paper mingled with the smell from the brazier, causing Suguro's nausea to churn all the more inside him.

'Suguro, it looks like I lost out.'

He somehow found the strength to answer despite his headache and fatigue.

'Lost out? What do you mean, Doctor?'

'Why, that ward patient died before I could get to her. I was going to try that new method.'

'You feel like a fish has run off with your bait, Doctor?' asked Toda drily.

'No, more like the feeling of having lost at love, isn't that it, Doctor?' interposed Asai's feminine voice from over by the window.

'Why can't they come to the point?' thought Suguro choking back the nausea aggravated by the smoke from the brazier.

Shibata idly picked up one of the tea cups and placed it on his up-turned palm. He lowered his eyes and began to turn it round and round.

'Well. . . . At any rate, in a day or two, you'll be hearing something from the Old Man himself. Actually. . . .' His words came out almost with reluctance. 'Actually, we talked at length about whether or not it would be good to have you two participate.'

After saying this much, he stopped talking and once more began to twirl the cup on his palm. Suguro wiped off the sweat which had gathered on his forehead. The flames danced up from the charcoal fire, and a smell like rotten fish floated through the room.

'Actually, on the whole, it seems better that you don't.

74

But for a medical research man, from one point of view that is, it is the most sought after kind of opportunity.'

The loud squeak of the chair, whose need of oil was apparent, continued to accompany the cup twirling.

'Both of you know, I suppose, that ever since *that* operation, the Old Man feels that Second Surgery and Doctor Kando have gained the upper hand. Now this time, we feel that getting on good terms ourselves with the Western Command medical people, with whom Second is so cosy, wouldn't be a bad idea at all. Therefore we feel there's no need to ill-temperedly refuse their friendly proposal and hurt their feelings. Of course, however, if the work seems distasteful to you, that'll have to end it for us. Five doctors from Kando's section most likely will be glad to get the chance. But with you two, myself, Asai here, and the Old Man – five of us can do it well enough.'

'It's an operation?' Toda asked. 'All you have to do, Doctor, is say the word and we take part.'

'No, no! No forcing. However, even if you don't take part, I'll have to ask you two to keep your mouths shut about it completely.'

'What kind of operation is it?'

'There are going to be some vivisections performed on American prisoners, Toda.'

When Suguro opened his eyes in the blackness, he heard the distant roar of the sea, the dark mass of the sea surging up over the shore, then the same dark mass falling back again.

'Why did I have to get involved in that vivisection business? I didn't have a fair chance. If it had only occurred to me to refuse there in Dr Shibata's room, I would have refused.'

His keeping quiet and assenting – was it because he was drawn along by Toda? Or was it because of his headache and the nausea churning in the pit of his stomach? And then the blue charcoal flames and the smell of Toda's cigarette had made him all the more faint and listless.

'How about it Suguro?' His rimless glasses shining, Asai leaned his face close. 'You're perfectly free, you know. Really.'

Afterwards, the short, plump medical officer had returned to the room and laughed, 'The bastards, what did they do but bomb indiscriminately? They've already been sentenced to be shot by the Western Command. Wherever they're executed it's the same. Why, here they'll get ether and die in their sleep!'

'It's all the same,' Suguro kept thinking. 'I was drawn into it because of the blue charcoal flames maybe. Maybe because of Toda's cigarette. Because of one thing, because of another, what does it matter? It's all the same. Thinking. Sleeping. No matter how much you think, it doesn't help. I'm just one person. What can I do with the world?' Suguro would fall asleep; then his eyes would open again. And once more he would fall into a gloomy doze. In his dreams he saw himself in the dark sea, his figure a battered husk swept round in the current.

From that day on, whenever Suguro and Toda happened to face each other in the laboratory, they avoided each other's eyes. When the topics they discussed began to drift towards the threatening vortex, one or the other would quickly change the subject. Why they had acquiesced to Dr Shibata's proposal, neither of them explained to the other. When others discussed the operations, both of them went about their work with strained faces.

The assignment sheet for the vivisections came out the day before the first of them and it was secretly distributed by Asai. On the first day of First Surgery's project, three prisoners were scheduled for operations. The aims of the vivisection experiment were described as follows:

1. Normal saline is to be injected into the blood stream of the first prisoner. The possible quantitative limits of such a procedure before death occurs are to be ascertained.
2. Air is to be injected into the veins of the second prisoner and the volume at which death occurs is to be ascertained.
3. There is to be an excision of the lung of the third prisoner. The limit to which the bronchial tubes may be cut before death occurs is to be ascertained.

Surgeons: Professor Hashimoto, Professor Shibata (Assistant)
First Assistant: Hiroshi Asai
Second Assistant: Tsuyoshi Toda
Third Assistant: Jiro Suguro

The experiment to be performed on the first prisoner was of great relevance to medical practice in wartime. The normal saline was made by dissolving 0.95 grams of salt in 100 c.c. of distilled water. Exactly how much of this solution could be safely injected as a substitute for blood into the blood of a patient had not been determined. Since a human life was always at stake in this procedure, the question was still a moot point. The general view was that something between one and two litres was safe, but beyond that nothing was known.

The second experiment consisted of inserting air into the veins of a prisoner. If 500 c.c. of air was inserted into a rabbit, the result was instant death. But what about a man?

The experiment with the third prisoner involved a problem which surgeons were especially eager to solve. Doctor

Sekiguchi of Tohoku University and Doctor Osawa of Osaka Imperial University had devised an extremely promising method of excising a lung, but the problem that remained concerned the extent to which the bronchial tubes could safely be cut.

As Suguro read the summary, he realized at once that Shibata, not the Old Man, had been behind the plan for the first two experiments. Blinking as always, he thought of the hollow-cheeked face of Dr Shibata.

The following day was the one preceding the operations. That evening Suguro, no longer fighting with the question 'Why?' devoted himself to cleaning out the drawers of his desk and arranging the things he kept on top of it. Toda took in this activity while smoking a cigarette.

'I'm going home. You?' Suguro asked.

'No.' Toda's voice was hollow as he answered.

'Good night.'

'Wait a second.' Toda got up suddenly and stopped Suguro at the door.

'What?'

'Just sit down a minute.'

Suguro sat down, but nothing was said. To speak would be to lie, Suguro thought. He felt that Toda was laughing at him.

'Have a cigarette.'

Toda held out to Suguro the celluloid case containing the ineptly rolled cigarettes which were his handiwork. Suguro took one, lit it, and then gazed at the blazing tip – gazing and saying nothing. 'You're another fool,' Toda muttered.

'Uh.'

'If you think you should have refused, you still have time to do it.'

'Uh.'

'Will you refuse?'

'I suppose not.'

'Do you think there's a God?'

'A God?'

'Oh what the hell, Suguro! Well, let me give it a try. Look, a man has all sorts of things pushing him. He tries by all means to get away from fate. Now the one who gives him the freedom to do that, you can call God.'

Suguro sighed. 'I don't know what you're talking about.' The glowing tip had gone out, and Suguro laid the cigarette down on the desk top. 'For myself, I can't see how whether there's a God or whether there's not a God makes any difference.'

'Yes, that's right. But for you maybe the old lady was a kind of God.'

'Yes, maybe.'

He got up and carrying his instrument case went out into the corridor. Toda did not stop him this time.

PART TWO

Those to Be Judged

1 · The Nurse

Problems at home prevented me from finishing my course at Fukuoka Nurses Training School until I was twenty-five. Then I started to work in the hospital of the Medical School. That year there was somebody I knew named Ueda who was in the hospital for an appendicectomy. I want to forget about Ueda and since, except for one thing, married life with him doesn't have anything to do with this matter, I'm not going to write about it in detail here. When I think of that man, I always remember a very hot day in early autumn with the sun streaming in at the window of his second floor room and him lying on the bed in a crepe shirt and a pair of undershorts that reached to his knees. He was short and pot-bellied, and he sweated a lot, always overcome by the heat. One of my duties as his nurse was to wipe off this sweat. At that time I had no particular liking or curiosity towards this man with the narrow, sleepy, little eyes.

One day Ueda all of a sudden rubbed his face against my stomach and grabbed my hand and held on to it. Even now I don't know why I let him do it. I think it suddenly flashed through my mind that twenty-five was starting to get on a bit as far as marriage was concerned, and then, too, his job as a clerk with Manchurian Railways wasn't a bad position, I thought to myself. And then – this is a bit embarrassing – but at that time I really wanted very much to have a baby. Not just anybody's baby, of course; but having a baby by somebody like Ueda would be all right I thought.

Outside the hospital the cicadas were making an awful noise. His hand was dripping with sweat.

Ueda's family lived in Osaka; so the wedding was held in Fukuoka, in the Yakuin area, where my brother lived. I can clearly remember Ueda, in a rented dress suit that was too short, wiping the sweat off his fat neck all through the ceremony. As soon as the wedding was over, we went to the port of Shimonoseki, where we got on a boat going to Dairen. Ueda had been reassigned from the branch office in Fukuoka to the home office of Manchurian Railways in Dairen. The boat was called the *Midori Maru*, and the third class quarters we were in were packed with farmers heading for Manchuria. There was an awful smell of fish oil and *takuan* coming from where they did their cooking. To me who had never done anything like leaving Shimonoseki and going to a foreign place, the whole idea of crossing the sea and going to this Kanto colony, which I knew nothing about, was pretty upsetting. 1 sat on the matting which was spread over the floor and thought and thought. When I looked at the faces of the farmers' families – they were lying on top of old trunks and wicker baskets – I got the feeling that I too was leaving the home country and going all by myself to work in a far-away place. At night all of them would sing these war songs they liked very loudly. And Ueda, even though I was really seasick, wanted to get romantic.

'Don't! Let me go!' I was embarrassed with all the people around, and I pushed his fat body away. 'Why did you have to come back third class? The company gave you the money for the return trip, didn't they?'

'Once we get to Dairen we're going to have to buy all kinds of things. What's the sense of wasting money before that?'

Then his piggy little eyes got all the narrower as he looked me over in what was supposed to be a tender way.

84

'You feel like vomiting? It can't be *that*! It's a bit early for that, I think,' he said.

All day long the black surface of the East China Sea rose and fell, slanting back and forth outside the porthole. As I watched the sea with nothing at all in mind, the thought came to me: 'Well, this is married life for you.'

On the morning of the fourth day we arrived at Dairen harbour. Rain mixed with coal dust dripped from the roofs of the warehouses. Some Chinese coolies came up the gang-plank, ordered around by soldiers with guns at their hips. They were carrying big sacks on their backs, swaying from side to side on their skinny legs.

'Those bastards! It only takes two of them to carry a piano.' Ueda stood with his face to the porthole, fingering my earlobe.

A lot of carts pulled by long-eared mules were lined up on the pier waiting for the passengers.

'Those aren't mules, you know. They're Manchurian horses.'

Before he came to Fukuoka four years before, Ueda had worked at the Dairen main office, and now he was proud of being able to tell me all about everything we saw on the way from the pier to the company housing area.

'This is Sanken Street. That's Oyama Street. All the big streets are named after generals and admirals of the Russian War.'

'Will we have to have anything to do with the Chinese?' I asked holding on to Ueda's sweaty hand. I told myself that in this city there was no one I had to depend upon but him.

The place where we were to live was right by the main temple in Dairen. Winter was cold here, so the houses weren't made of wood. Our little house was built of dark coloured brick. All around were lots of others just like it. None of them had more than two rooms. But they had built into the wall an unusual kind of heating system called a *pechika*.

At the beginning I thought that this colonial town was really strange. The well kept acacia trees which lined the streets and the Russian style buildings looked quite different from the flimsy houses of an ordinary Japanese town. Everybody – soldiers or ordinary people too, as long as they were Japanese – walked fast and were bursting with energy.

'Where do the Manchurians live?' I asked Ueda.

'On the edge of town,' he answered laughing. 'It's a dirty place. It stinks of garlic. You wouldn't want to go there.'

About this time at home, rationing had started to become pretty strict. So I was surprised to see how cheap things were here and how much there was of everything.

'Lady, how about some fish?' Every morning Chinese selling fresh fish and vegetables would shout at me, undercutting each other's prices as much as they could. For only ten *sen* you could buy one or two big Ise crabs.

'Dammit! These bastards take you in every time. You don't go about it right at all.' Ueda would take a look at the account book every morning and usually give me a lecture.

Within less than two months of coming to this place, I realized how right Ueda was when he said that the first thing for a Japanese to learn here was the proper way of acting towards the Manchurians. For example, next door to us lived the Zoga family, and they had two Manchurians, boys of fifteen and sixteen, as servants. From across the garden I could hear Mrs Zoga and her husband yelling at them and hitting them. At first all this racket scared me, but gradually I got used to it. Ueda told me that it was the way these Manchurians were. You had to knock them around; otherwise they wouldn't do anything. Then it happened that in place of a maid I started having a girl come in three times a week. And, sure enough, I soon got into the habit of hitting her, for no reason at all.

What with the cheap prices and the prettiness of the city and the life being better than at home, I was fairly contented. I thought at the time that this meant I was contented with Ueda. The first winter came. It was December. The inside of the room was kept much warmer than that of a Japanese house by the *pechika,* but anything that got a bit damp, whether it was a tangerine or a shoe, quickly got as hard as a rock. While waiting for Ueda to come home – he was often late, on company business as he said – I would spend the winter evenings sewing baby clothes – I was pregnant – and having my hips massaged by the girl. Outside, through the falling snow, you could hear the sound of cartwheels a long way off and the driver using his whip on the horses.

Innocent as I was, I had no idea that Ueda was often spending his evenings at the place of a woman who worked in a restaurant called the Iroha in the Naniwa district. The one who first let me in on this was Mrs Zoga next door. My first reaction was, 'It can't be true!' When I asked Ueda, he just narrowed his piggy eyes and laughed. When I was laughed at, I wanted to believe it was true. But in the dark of the night when I felt his hands on me, my body wouldn't listen to the cruel thing my heart had to say, and I couldn't doubt my husband then.

It was April, already spring at home, but in Dairen there was still snow piled up, blackened by the smoke from kerosene stoves. The cold was still sharp, and I was in the hospital run by Manchurian Railways waiting for the birth of my baby. Since this hospital was almost free of charge to the families of employees of Manchurian Railways, Ueda urged me to enter it as early as I wanted since this was

87

'profitable', and I took what he had to say in good faith. I never even dreamed that he who wanted the baby so much too, once he got his wife into hospital, would bring the other woman to live at the house with him.

Even today to write about the birth is painful, seeing that I have to bring it all up again. When you read this account, maybe you'll see that it's because it turned out that I was never to have a child, that there is something missing in my heart and in my life. For some reason or other, the baby died inside me. I had chosen the name Masuo for my baby and was happy about it, but it turned out that I wasn't able to get even a look at his face or his body. As a nurse I knew how most of these stillbirths turned out, but I cried and begged the doctor to see him, but it was no use. And finally in order to save my life, it was necessary to cut out my womb altogether.

'Nothing to worry about,' said Ueda, looking at me with his narrow piggy eyes. Now that I think of it, he was probably happy from the bottom of his heart about the death of the baby because now it was easier to get rid of me. 'I asked the doctor. He said everything would be O.K. What? About the operation? Almost no expense. It's practically all taken care of by the Company. It's no big loss.'

When I heard him say this, I thought at once: 'He's got himself another woman, hasn't he?' Mrs Zoga had been right. But funnily enough, I didn't get mad at him or feel jealous. When they took away my womanhood, I had a feeling as if a pit had broken open at my feet – and that empty feeling just swallowed me up. If I had been turned into stone, it would have come to the same thing. Some women have an operation to help them. But my womanhood was torn from me, and there was nothing else for it but to go through life a crippled woman.

When I left the hospital about a month later, I noticed when I came out into the street that at last it was spring in Dairen too. At the street corners willow trees were blooming, and their blossoms were like cotton balls, all being blown around by the wind. Some of these white petals stuck to Ueda's sweaty neck. He had come to take me home. The petals floated down on the trunk which the Chinese girl had brought. I bit my lips and shuddered when I remembered that it contained the useless nappies and baby clothes.

Two years after that Ueda and I broke up. When he told me, I did the usual screaming and crying, but it would make this account too long if I went into the whole boring business, and so I'll just leave it out.

Funnily enough, I can't remember anything special that happened during that last two years with him. When I force myself to think about it, all I can remember is him getting fatter and fatter and daily taking some kind of brown-coloured liquid medicine because he was worried about his blood pressure. He told me that having sex was bad for his heart, and so he would often come home late and be asleep and snoring in no time. Actually I knew the truth of the matter was that the woman at the Iroha had taken everything out of him. In the dark whenever his big, hot body rolled over near me, I'd push it away. It wasn't just that I didn't really love him any more. Even physically I didn't really want him. Not being able to have a child seemed to have stopped me wanting sex. Even so for two years I kept on living with him on account of my own weakness and because of what people would say. I just didn't want to become one of those poor women – there were so many of them – who were kicked out by their husbands and had to go back home.

When I left him, I said goodbye to Dairen from the deck

of the same *Midori Maru* of three years before. Just as on the day I came, sooty rain was dripping from the warehouse roofs, and military police were herding coolies carrying heavy sacks up the gangplank. When I thought to myself that I'd never see this sort of thing again, or the city itself, I felt even more as if a big weight was off my mind.

When I got back to Fukuoka, the War had already broken out in the South Pacific, and the town was filled with soldiers and workers. But whenever life became a bit tough, I just thought of what I had gone through in Dairen and then there was as much difference as between heaven and hell. My brother and sister-in-law weren't especially happy to see me back, and since I'm not the kind to put up with anything, I got mad, took a job as a nurse at the hospital, and left their house. I rented a room in a small apartment house not far from the Medical school. At the hospital the faces of the nurses and of the medical department people were all changed from those I had known four years before, the time I got to know Ueda so well there. All the former interns were now doctors and medical officers somewhere in the Army or Navy, and the nurses who were my classmates had gone off as military nurses to the war zones. I had never dreamed when I was in Dairen that the War would already have such an effect so close to the hospital. The head of First Surgery, Dr Inoue, had died, and now Dr Hashimoto had taken his place, I found out. Now that I had broken up with Ueda, I had made up my mind to live my life and put up with whatever came my way, but even so, starting to work in the hospital again wasn't so enjoyable. The nurses who had been way behind me in the Nursing School now walked through the hallways as though they owned the place and gave me orders. Then, too, I knew that rumours about me, my coming back from Manchuria and everything, were very popular in the night duty room. I got permission from my landlord and bought a little mongrel bitch. I knew how extravagant this was at a time when food was getting harder and harder to get, but to have some living thing with me, even a dog, was a sort of consolation in my lonely life. I called the dog Masu, and I was thinking of the dead baby in Dairen, Masuo. When you yelled at her, she'd start trembling, and if she did something wrong, she'd run to a corner of the room to hide. She was the only outlet I had now for my affection.

But at night in the darkness when for some reason or other I'd wake up a bit and hear that roaring of the waves in the dark – the ocean wasn't so far from the flat – I'd suddenly be hit by a kind of indescribable loneliness. Without knowing it I'd put my hand outside the quilt as though I was reaching for something. When I realized that I was looking for Ueda, whom I should have forgotten completely, I'd start crying, feeling sorry for myself. What I really thought at those times was how much I wanted someone to come and live with me.

Now in this account I don't feel like writing anything which might seem to be in my own defence, but actually all during this time, the Chief Surgeon, Dr Hashimoto, meant nothing to me except insofar as he was the man in charge of the work I did. I was just a nurse, and to me professors and assistant professors were not just on the great master level but were people who right from the day they were born, lived in a different world. The position we nurses have is just a little above scrub women. And so, funnily enough, the one thing that ties me up with Dr Hashimoto is his wife, Hilda.

Mrs Hilda was a nurse when Dr Hashimoto was studying in Germany. I remember hearing the story of their romance when I was a student nurse. The first time I saw her, though, was two weeks after I started to work at the hospital again. It was in the late afternoon. A well-built European woman suddenly appeared at the entrance of First Surgery, pushing a bicycle with a big basket strapped to it. To my surprise all the nurses snapped to attention and came running, and this foreign woman with short hair and wearing slacks walked right into the hospital. You got the feeling that she was a strong young man rather than a woman.

'Who's that?' I asked a young nurse named Konno who was standing beside me.

'You don't know?' She shrugged her shoulders at my ignorance. 'That's Mrs Hilda, the chief surgeon's wife.'

Mrs Hilda took a cellophane wrapped package from the big basket and handed it to Dr Asai. Dr Asai took it, smiling for all that he was worth. With all she had inside her blouse and her height, she seemed to overpower Dr Asai, even though he was a man. I saw, when she turned in my direction, that she used too much rouge. She waved to us and then taking big, mannish steps she went down the corridor. Inside the cellophane package she gave Dr Asai, there was a big stack of home-made biscuits. At that time you couldn't get biscuits and things like that anywhere, and so there was a mad scramble for them. I managed to get one.

As I ate it, I didn't say a word, waiting to see what the other nurses would have to say about Mrs Hilda. They chattered away about how thick her rouge was, something a Japanese woman certainly couldn't get away with. Then one said: 'She's really something isn't she? Passing out biscuits and washing underwear – that's her speciality.'

Afterwards I realized that they were being catty about her visit to the ward patients every time she came to the hospital. She came regularly three times a month. Carrying her biscuits, she'd go in to the wards. She'd get together all their dirty underwear, and then the next time she came she'd pass it out again all washed and clean. This was the 'work of devotion' that she had chosen.

The fact is that we nurses didn't appreciate her goodness very much. I think it was a lot of trouble to the ward patients too. The ward was filled with old men and women who had lost everyone they could depend on in the air raids, but to have a Western woman like this talk to them would cause them to freeze up. On top of it, when Mrs Hilda would pull out of their old cloth packs and wicker baskets their dirty underwear, they would get all upset and come crawling out of their beds.

'No, no, Ma'am. No, please! It's all right,' they'd plead.

The funny thing is that the patients' embarrassment didn't worry her a bit. Like a big boy, she'd take these great strides through the hospital, passing out her biscuits and rushing the patients to give up their dirty things so she could put them in her basket and move on to the next one.

Since I wrote all that in a catty way, I should say that all during that time I didn't really have any feeling against the goodwill activity she was carrying on.

'No doubt about it, you have to hand it to her. Today Mrs Hashimoto cleaned Fusa Ono's urine bottle. And she a European lady!' Dr Asai said in a voice which seemed all overflowing with emotion. To us nurses she was just 'really something', that's all. Beyond that we had no special reason to feel any dislike towards her.

The first time I did feel badly towards this woman was on account of something else.

It was an ordinary kind of late summer afternoon. I had

93

sat down on the steps leading to the garden and was just sitting there with my head in my hands. I was thinking about the time I was in that hospital run by Manchurian Railways in Dairen. About my baby's death.

Just at that moment, a little boy of about four or five came running out from the shadow of the building. His face was Japanese but his hair was light brown. I knew right away that this must be the son of Mrs Hilda and Dr Hashimoto. I felt something stirring inside me. If my boy had lived, that's just about how big he'd be. Without thinking, I stretched my hand out to the boy.

'Please don't touch him.'

All at once from behind me, I heard the stern voice of his mother. Mrs Hilda, rouge as thick as ever, was standing right over me with a hard expression on her face. Then, as if she was calling a dog, she whistled to the child.

But the child looked at me and then towards Mrs Hilda, as if he didn't know which way to go for a minute or two. Mrs Hilda and I both glared at each other as though we were gambling for the boy's affection. Why did I get so worked up? The painful memory of the day of my baby's birth and my being made something less than a woman was eating away at me. I felt all the bitterness you might have expected me to feel towards a happy wife and mother.

'Excuse me, please.' Hugging the child, Hilda spoke in fluent Japanese. 'As you know, children can get tuberculosis easily. When I leave the hospital, I always wash my hands with antiseptic.'

That night at my apartment, I felt my loneliness more than ever. When I was feeding the dog, I noticed her stomach was smeared with blood. Suddenly I got mad and lifted my hand, and, even though she crouched in a frightened way and looked pitifully at me with her eyes, I hit her over the head again and again. While I was hitting her, for some reason or other I didn't cry.

Suddenly I began to take an interest in Dr Hashimoto, but of course I wasn't interested in him because he was somebody on a higher level but rather because he was the husband of this Hilda. When this old man walked past the nurses lined up in front of the patients' rooms, dressed in his white coat, I didn't miss the fact that there was a little piece of tobacco sticking to his coat. More grey began to appear in his hair. His face was old and tired. The flesh of his cheeks was loose. How could Hilda, who was like a young athlete, love somebody like this? When I saw him touch a patient's chest with the tip of his finger, I would imagine that finger caressing Hilda. When I saw that one of his shirt buttons had been torn, I felt a secret happiness. I had noticed something which his wife, Hilda, had missed.

The War gradually became worse and worse. My flat, like the hospital itself, was pretty far from the city; so there wasn't any damage at all. Fukuoka itself was more than half burnt out with all the air raids. My brother who had lived in Yakuin near the centre of the city, had moved out into the country about six months before, but I never thought about going to visit him. And there were no visits from his side either. I heard a story about Ueda moving from Dairen to Harbin, but I never got so much as a post-card from him. I was a woman all by myself with no one in the world to depend upon, and I didn't even have any idea how the War was going, since I never felt like reading the newspapers. To tell the truth, I wasn't interested in whether my country won or whether it lost. About this time, when I opened my eyes at night in the dark, it seemed to me some-how that the sound of the sea was getting louder. As I strained my ears in the darkness, it seemed that last night more than the night before and tonight more than last night the noise of the waves was getting louder and louder. I thought of the War only at those times. As that sound, big and heavy like a bass drum, got louder and deeper, I thought: 'Japan's going to lose. And then where will we all be dragged off to?'

Dragged off anywhere, it didn't matter. More and more patients were dying at the hospital. Especially those in the TB wards. Like clockwork, one died every two weeks. You've got to have good nourishment with this sickness, and eventually these patients would have no more money to buy food on the black market. But no matter how many died, there was such an overflow of patients that as soon as a bed became empty, it would be filled again. Since I was a newcomer, I was assigned to this TB ward, but I didn't feel like taking care of the people lying there the way that Hilda did. I just did what I had to and beyond that not a thing. At any rate, whatever I might have done, I think my heart was just overwhelmed by the feeling of helplessness. It was as though everybody was being dragged through the middle of a dark ocean. I think that the second incident that occurred between Hilda and me was probably due to this mood of mine. There was an operation taking place on the young married woman who was in the second floor private room, so the nurses' room was empty except for me. Mrs Hilda had just arrived at the hospital but this time no one went to meet her at the door. I was alone in the duty room checking a blood pressure chart.

'Nurse, would you come here a minute?'

An old man from the ward, in a ragged nightgown, had stuck his head in at the door.

'Mrs Maebashi's having a bad time of it.'

'What's the trouble?'

'Don't know, but she's having a bad time of it.'

When I went to the ward, I found a woman patient called Maebashi with five or six others around her. She was in pain and grabbing at her chest with her eyes twitching. Being a nurse, I could tell by looking at her that she had an attack of spontaneous pneumothorax. Air was pouring into her pleural cavity and it was dangerous. I ran to the laboratory, but Dr Asai, Toda, and Suguro were all taking part in the operation. Only Dr Shibata was free, but I didn't see him anywhere either. I knew that unless the air was stopped, she would die of suffocation; so I called the operating theatre on the phone.

'Doctor Asai.' I spoke quickly to the nurse, Miss Konno, who picked up the receiver. 'A patient has a spontaneous pneumothorax. Let me talk to him.'

I don't know why, but through the receiver you could hear the sound of sandals scuffling quickly to and fro. It was a strange feeling, but it seemed to me that it was much quieter than a normal operation, as though something was wrong.

'What is it?' All at once I heard Dr Asai's angry voice in the receiver at my ear. He seemed very excited.

'A ward patient, Toki Maebashi, has a spontaneous pneumothorax.'

'There's nothing I can do. I'm busy. Do what you can.'

'But she's suffering terribly. . . .'

'Anyway she's past help. Give her a shot of anaesthetic. . . .'

I didn't hear any more because Dr Asai had slammed down the receiver. Give her a shot of anaesthetic, I thought. Give her a shot of anaesthetic. She's past help, I could hear his voice saying that inside me.

The late afternoon sun was pouring in through the window of the laboratory, and there was grey dust spread

over the tops of the desks. I picked up the bottle containing
the procaine liquid used as anaesthetic and a hypodermic
needle and went back to the ward. When I came in, I saw
Hilda beside the woman's bed holding on to its frame. She
was wearing slacks.

'Nurse, the pneumothorax equipment, quick!' she yelled
at me. Since she had been a nurse in a German hospital,
she knew at once that the woman had a spontaneous
pneumothorax. Then suddenly she stared at the bottle of
procaine and the needle I was carrying, and her face
changed colour. She knocked me to one side and rushed out
of the ward to look for the pneumothorax machine.

As I gathered together the shattered pieces of the bottle
on the floor, I could feel the stares of the patients on my
back. I went back to the nurses' room. The sun was just
going down in the distance. It was big, red and glowing,
just as it used to look in Dairen when I used to watch it
go down from my room in the Manchurian Railways
Hospital.

'Why were you about to give her an injection?' Hilda
stood at the door, her arms folded like a man, and angrily
cross-examined me. 'She was dying anyway, I suppose?
Was that it?'

'But. . . .' I looked down at the floor. 'Whatever I did,
she was going to die. Can't you help a person by letting
them die easier?'

'Even though a person is going to die, no one has the
right to murder him. You're not afraid of God? You don't
believe in the punishment of God?'

Mrs Hilda pounded the desk with her right hand. From
her blouse I could smell the scent of soap. Japanese like
us had no way of getting soap, the way things were then. It
was the same soap she used to wash the clothes and underwear of the ward patients. I don't know why, but some-

thing struck me as funny all of a sudden. Was it because of the soap, too, that the hand she pounded the desk with was so rough and chapped? You had the feeling of it having been rubbed with sand. I had no idea that the skin of white people got so dirty. The back of the hand was covered with little blond hairs. It all seemed so funny at first, but then as I listened, what she said began to get on my nerves. It was as though within me the thudding drumbeat of the sea roar I heard at night was getting louder and deeper.

That night I was on duty. I left the hospital in the middle of the night and was about to go back to my flat when I ran into Dr Asai, who was walking around outside.

'Doctor, how was the operation?'

'Who's that? You? Oh. What do you want?'

He had been drinking. So much so that he who always made such a fuss about his appearance had let his glasses slip down to the tip of his nose.

'We killed her.'

'She died?'

'Yes, yes, we did. The family doesn't know a thing yet, see. The Old Man – he just doesn't have it any more. The Old Man. . . . When the election comes off, old Kando will beat him hollow. And at a humbler level, you see, there goes my future too.'

He put his hand on my shoulder. I could smell wine on his breath as he staggered a little.

'Where do you live? I'll see you home.'

'It's just close by.'

'O.K. if I come?'

That night Dr Asai stayed in my room. I didn't mind at all.

'So you have a dog, uh? Hilda has a dog too. Hilda. She barged in again today, didn't she?'

'But, Doctor, you have so much respect for her.'

'Respect for her, eh? Just for the fun of it, I'd like to sleep with that white woman once.'

'I wonder how she is in bed with Dr Hashimoto?'

'Who, Hilda? Why she really gives, I'll bet. She's a woman underneath the plaster saint business. Just look at her body! Hey, why don't you try your luck with Dr Hashimoto? That would really fix old Hilda!'

I felt Dr Asai's hands on me, but there was no pleasure in it at all. I had my eyes closed, and I was wondering how Dr Hashimoto would go about telling Hilda that today he had killed a patient in an operation. I thought of Hilda's white hands and of the scent of soap coming from her blouse. It was only to fight against that scent that I gave myself to Dr Asai.

The next day when I went to the hospital, Dr Asai, very different from the night before, called me over to him with a cold look on his face.

'Ueda, what have you been up to with the ward patients?'

'The ward patients, Doctor?'

'There was a woman with a spontaneous pneumothorax wasn't there? I got a phone call from Mrs Hilda. She stopped you from doing something, she said.'

'All I was going to do, Doctor, was what you –'

'Me? I didn't say anything!'

As I looked at him, the light shining from those rimless glasses, he suddenly became flustered and looked away. This was the man who had so ardently wrapped himself around me the night before.

'Should I give notice?'

'Nobody said anything about giving notice, Ueda.'

He put on one of those charming smiles he was so good at.

'But look, when Frau Hilda comes to the hospital, it

might be a bit awkward, you see. Take about a month off, eh? After that leave it to me to fix everything up.'

That evening when I returned to the flat, I couldn't find Masu anywhere. I asked the landlord, but he just shook his head. It was around this time that people were getting so hungry that they were even killing and eating dogs. Someone probably came and took her while I was out. I sat down for a while on the step to my room and just stared. I felt I didn't care what happened from then on. I didn't care about Dr Asai. I was thinking about Hilda, who called up wanting them to fire me. I hated her. Just so she could play the saint all by herself, she didn't care at all how much trouble she gave the patients and the nurses. For her, a saint and a mother, somebody like me, who had everything that made her a woman taken out of her, sleeping with Dr Asai would be something dirty, I suppose. What was I going to do now that even Masu was gone?

It was terribly hard staying away from the hospital for a month all by myself in my room. When I was working, I could get away from the old thoughts about Dairen, about waiting for the baby. But when there was nothing to do but lie there on the mat, I couldn't do anything but go over again and again in my mind about the day of my baby's death, and the day I was thrown out by Ueda. I even thought that I would be glad to see Ueda again.

Then one night, Dr Asai came again.

'I've got a little matter to talk over with you.'

'I've been fired.'

'No.' With a tense look on his face, Dr Asai sat down cross-legged on the mat. 'This is about something more serious.'

'To me there's nothing more serious than getting fired.'

'Look, as far as that goes, I want you back at the hospital.'

'You want me to help you with something, eh? There's something that somebody like me can help out with? If you want a nurse to kill patients, here I am.'

That was the night that I heard about the operations on the American prisoners. The chief surgeon himself, Dr Hashimoto, and Dr Shibata and the two interns, Dr Suguro and Dr Toda, were going to take part; but there was no nurse yet, he said.

'So you've come to me!' I laughed – it was almost like a spasm.

'Now, don't take it like that. This is for your country's sake. They've all been condemned to death anyway. This way they can do some good for the advancement of medical science.' Dr Asai gave me all the reasons he didn't believe himself. Then in an embarrassed voice:

'Will you do it?'

'Doing it for my country doesn't mean a thing to me. Neither does doing it for your medical research.'

I didn't care whether Japan won the war or lost it. And I didn't care whether medical science advanced or not. It was all the same to me.

'I wonder if the chief surgeon told Mrs Hilda about this business.'

'Don't joke. And don't go saying anything to anybody about it. Not a word, understand?'

I thought of what Hilda said when she was yelling at me that afternoon in the nurses' room, about not being afraid of God, and I laughed to myself. It was a feeling a little like that of winning. She, after all, didn't know what her husband was doing, but I did.

'Mrs Hilda, no. How could the chief surgeon ever tell saintly Mrs Hilda about it?'

That night in Dr Asai's arms, I opened my eyes, and I could hear a gloomy, deep drumming noise – the roaring of

102

the sea again. And the scent of Mrs Hilda's soap came back
to me again. Her right hand – a Western woman's skin with
the downy hair growing on it. I thought: soon a scalpel is
going to cut into white skin just like that.

'Is a white person's skin hard to cut, I wonder?'

'What? Don't be silly. Foreigner, Japanese – it's just the
same,' Dr Asai muttered as he rolled over.

If my baby hadn't died in Dairen, if I hadn't broken up
with Ueda, my life wouldn't have been like this, I kept
thinking.

2 · An Intern

About 1935 in Rokko Elementary School on the eastern
edge of Kobé, there was only one pupil with long hair, and
that was me. Now the district has become a large residential area, but at that time the school was surrounded
with onion fields and farmhouses. And the Hankyu trains
going to Osaka and back would have these fields to either
side of them. Most of the pupils were the children of
farmers. No lads like me with long hair. Among the mass of
bald, shaven heads, were many boys who came to school
with babies strapped to their backs. The babies would wet
their nappies during class and start to set up a howl, upsetting the young teachers no end.

'Take him outside,' they'd say, pointing to the corridor.

The way the boys were addressed was different from
Tokyo. It was always the first name, Maseru Tsutomu, or
whatever it was. Only when I was called on in class, was
there a difference. Then it was always 'Master Toda'. The

103

pupils made the same distinction as did the teachers, and it wasn't considered a bit strange. This was due to my being the only one who wasn't a farmer's son. My father was a doctor, and he had opened a surgery not far from the school. And these teachers, with their tight-collared jackets, were no doubt in awe of a great personage like a doctor and of the plate with M.D. on it. At any rate, I wasn't a very strong boy, but right from the beginning, I got nothing but A's on my report card, and I was the only boy in the school who was going to continue his education. Every school year, I took the leading role in the plays, entertainments, and so on. Then, too, when I drew pictures for the school exhibitions, I received the prize as a matter of course. Without going about it in a deliberate way, I made a practice of pulling the wool over the eyes of adults. These included not just my tight-collared teachers but also my mother and father. I didn't have any trouble reading their unsubtle eyes and facial expressions in order to estimate how best to make them happy or to extract praise from them, sometimes playing the innocent role, sometimes that of the bright child. I perceived by a sort of instinct exactly what adults wanted to see in me: a blend of naïveté and wisdom. Overplaying naïveté wouldn't do nor, on the other hand, would seeming too wise. However, if one doled out these commodities to adults in just the right measure, they would inevitably respond with praise. The me who is writing now, today, doesn't look upon the me of that time, the bright little boy, as having been especially crafty. I'd like you to think a bit about your own childhood. All bright children have more or less the same kind of slyness about them. And then it sometimes happens that they foster in themselves the congenial illusion that they are good children precisely because of this capacity.

On the first day of class of the second term, when I was

in the fifth form, the teacher came into the classroom with a small boy, who wore glasses and had a white band, the designation of a new pupil, wrapped around his head. He stood beside the teacher's dais hanging his head to one side like a girl, staring at a spot on the floor.

'Boys,' the young teacher in yellow-belted trousers addressed us in a loud voice, his hands on his hips, 'here's a new friend who has just changed schools from Tokyo. Treat him well. Otherwise you may regret it.'

Then he wrote on the blackboard the name Minoru Wakabayashi.

'You, Akira. Can you read this boy's name?'

There was some commotion in the classroom, and in the midst of it, many boys secretly looked my way. They did this because this boy Wakabayashi had long hair just like mine. I looked at him, the band wrapped round his head, with a feeling compounded more or less of hostility and jealousy. As he was pushing up his glasses which had slipped down his nose, he suddenly stole a glance at me and then quickly looked down again.

'Boys, you brought your compositions today on what you did during the summer, didn't you?' the teacher asked. 'Master Wakabayashi, sit at that desk and listen. First, Master Toda, read yours.'

To hear him say 'Master Wakabayashi' was a severe blow to my self esteem. That way of being addressed in this class had been up to today my exclusive privilege.

I got up as ordered and began to read my composition. I had always taken keen pleasure in this moment. To have my own composition as the model for all and to read it aloud before the world was a glorious sensation, but today I felt unsettled as I read. The glasses of the new pupil seated to one side of me got on my nerves. He came from a

105

Tokyo school. He had long hair. His collar was white, and his clothes were fashionable.

'I'm not going to lose out!' I muttered to myself.

When I wrote a composition, I always made it a point to put in two or three purple patches. For such vulgar embellishments were exactly what the young teachers just out of training college took the most delight in. I hadn't planned it in cold blood precisely, but in order to get praise from this particular young teacher, who had read us selections from Miekichi Suzuki's *The Red Bird*, I had concocted a scene meant to be evocative of naïve purity and boyish sentiment.

' "One day during the summer vacation, I heard that Master Kimura was sick, and so I thought that I would go to visit him." ' I began to read aloud in front of everyone. So much was true enough, but the part which followed was, characteristically, a piece of my own devising. As a present for the sick Master Kimura, I picked out a box of butterfly specimens, which I had gone to great efforts to collect, and started for his house. As I was walking through the onion fields, I was suddenly struck by misgivings about what I had decided to do. Any number of times, I was on the point of stopping and going back home; but finally I came to Master Kimura's house. Then after I had seen the expression of joy on his face, I felt great peace of heart, and so on.

'All right.' The teacher, with an expression of utter contentment on his face after I had finished reading, looked around at the faces of the boys in the class. 'Now what was especially good about Master Toda's composition? What part? Doesn't anybody know? Anybody who knows raise his hand.'

Two or three boys, full of self-confidence, put up their hands. What they answered and what the teacher was bursting to say turned out to be just what I had anticipated. It was true that I had brought a butterfly collection to a boy named Maseru Kimura, but it wasn't for the purpose of consoling him in sickness. It was true too that I had walked through the onion fields filled with chirping grass-hoppers, but I had never thought of regretting giving the collection to Kimura. Why? Because all I had to do was to ask my father and he would buy me three more just like it. Kimura wasn't especially delighted, and what I thought at the time was how dirty farmers let their houses get, and what I felt was a sense of superiority.

'Akira, tell us what you think.'

'I think that Master Toda giving that butterfly collection, something really valuable like that, to Maseru, was very generous.'

'Yes, yes, of course it was, but. . . . How about the good thing about the composition?'

Seizing the chalk the teacher began to write on the board. He wrote the three Chinese characters for *conscientious*.

'When he was walking through the onion fields, he felt sorry about giving the butterflies, and that's just the way he wrote it down. All of you sometimes put lies into your compositions. But Master Toda here has frankly written exactly how he felt. That's being conscientious.'

I gazed at the three figures on the board which signified *conscientious*. From a classroom somewhere, the faint sound of an organ could be heard. The girls' choir was practising. My conscience wasn't at all troubled about having lied or having deceived the teacher and my class-mates. This was the way I had always acted whether at school or at home. And by so doing, I had become known as a good boy and a first-class student.

I stole a sidelong glance at the long-haired new boy, who,

107

his glasses slipped down a bit on his nose, was staring fixedly at the blackboard. Did he feel my look? At any rate, he twisted his head with its white band and looked in my direction. For a few moments we looked at each other as though searching each other's face. His cheeks reddened a bit, and a thin smile played around his lips.

'You fooled them all, eh? But I know.' His smile seemed to be telling me just that. 'Walking through the onion fields, feeling sorry about giving the butterflies – all lies. You did it cleverly. But even though you put it over on adults, you don't fool a Tokyo boy.'

I looked away. I could feel the blood rushing up right to the tips of my ears. The organ stopped. The girls' voices were not singing any more. The figures on the blackboard wavered before my eyes.

From then on my self-confidence began, bit by bit, to crumble. As long as that boy, Wakabayashi, was near me, in the classroom or on the playground, I felt as though some intangible humiliation were hanging over me. Of course my marks did not go down at all because of this. But when I was praised in front of everybody by the teacher, when my handwriting or my pictures were put up on the wall, when my classmates chose me as a member of the school council, I would, with a sort of compulsion, steal a look at his eyes.

When I think now of the expression in his eyes, I know that they were by no means the eyes of an accusing judge; nor were they the eyes of conscience threatening punishment. It was no more than a matter of two boys sharing the same secret, in whom the same seed of evil was implanted – each of whom perceived in the other the image of himself. What I felt at that time were no pricks of conscience but rather the humiliation that comes of having another in on one's secret.

He played with nobody at all. During break when everyone else was playing ball, he stood off by himself in a corner of the schoolyard, leaning on a seesaw and staring in my direction. During calisthenics, too, his white-banded head could be seen in the distance as he stood looking on. When the boys talked to him, he gave unenthusiastic answers like, 'I don't care for it,' or 'I don't know.' Even though his hair was long like mine and he wore city clothes, as soon as the other boys realized that he was neither strong nor good at classwork, they began to make fun of his pale girlish face. Finally, I too lost my fear of him. I forgot about that first day's humiliation.

Then one day he was teased by two farmers' boys. I had just finished my after-school duties as a monitor, and was leaving the school building for home, when I saw two boys called Maseru and Susumu pulling his hair over by the sandpit. He struggled with them, but then he was hit and knocked down and lay face up in the sand. When he tried to get up, they knocked him down again. As I watched this scene, it never occurred to me to try to stop them. I didn't pity him at all. Rather I was wishing that Maseru and Susumu would hit him harder and pull his hair more. I hadn't noticed that a teacher had suddenly appeared at one of the windows, and so I stood there and watched the struggle for a few moments longer. But as soon as I became aware of the teacher coming down the hallway towards the entrance, I snapped into action at once and ran over to the sandpit.

'Cut it out! Cut it out!' Fully aware of the teacher's presence behind me, I shouted at the top of my voice. Maseru! You shouldn't tease a new boy. Wait till teacher comes!'

When Maseru and Susumu turned and saw the teacher coming, their faces turned red. The boy still lay in the sand.

'Master Wakabayashi, what happened? Are you all right?'

As the boy raised his face, the afternoon sun lit it and caught the grains of sand clinging to it. His glasses, their frames twisted, had fallen into the sand. When I went to brush the sand off his cheek with my hand, the boy suddenly turned his face away and knocked aside my hand as though it were an unclean thing.

'What, you still want to fight? Even though I stopped it for you?'

Without thinking I clenched my fists, but just at that moment I realized that the teacher was now beside me.

'Maseru again!' I muttered as though to myself.

'Now what's this all about, Master Toda?'

'Sir, Maseru, he. . . . Master Wakabayashi here. . . .' I stammered, unwontedly flustered. 'As soon as I saw it, I rushed over to stop it.'

Then, as I regained control and began one of my usual performances, the boy, the afternoon sun full in his face, looked neither at the teacher nor at me but stared vacantly in another direction. It was the first time I had seen his face without its glasses, and the uncanny feeling surged up in me that, no doubt about it, here was one person able to see to the bottom of my heart.

'You did a good job, Master Toda. You two! Maseru, Susumu! If you'd only be a little bit like your president. You see the way he. . . .'

'Your president' – that was me. While the simple-minded teacher scolded the culprits, the boy, not saying a word, brushed the sand from his face, picked up his canvas bag, which was lying on the ground, and walked away, like one in no way involved.

The following spring Wakabayashi changed schools again. That day, just as on the first, the teacher brought him, a white band around his head, to the front of the room and had him stand beside the dais. He wrote on the blackboard as he had on the first day, but this time the word he wrote was Ashio.

'Yoshimasa! What kind of place is Ashio?'

No response from Yoshimasa.

'Tomio?'

'Copper. It's a place where they mine copper.'

'That's right. These past few months, Master Wakabayashi became a good friend of ours, but now because of his father's work, his family is moving to Ashio. So today is the last day he'll be in this class.'

On occasions like this, the teacher became all at once the soul of gentle consideration. As for me, I thought about this boy going to the copper town of Ashio. Bare, treeless hills surrounded it and black smoke stacks dirtied the sky above it. There he would stand hanging his head like a girl looking down at the ground. Wrapped around his head, just like today, would be a white band.

'Master Toda, on behalf of the class, say goodbye to Master Wakabayashi,' said the teacher.

'Goodbye, Master Wakabayashi.'

He didn't say anything. But then as he was leaving the classroom at the end of the day, as though twisting that white head band, he suddenly turned, looking back towards me. One last time that faint smile of mockery curled his lips.

After that I forgot about him. At least I wanted to forget about him. For a while the desk where he had sat stood solitary and empty. But then the janitor took it away somewhere; and so there was nothing at all to remind me of him.

111

There was no need now to steal a look at that face. Once more I was the good boy. Once more I read my compositions in a loud, firm voice and received the teacher's praise.

The summer vacation came. One day around noon, when the heat was at its height, I was walking alone through the onion fields near the school. The grasshoppers were singing raspingly in the grass, and some distance down the path a man selling ice candy was pulling his squeaking cart.

All at once the thought of the composition I had written the summer before came back to me. I wrote that I had brought a butterfly collection to a sick boy named Kimura. I had written it for the express purpose of reading it aloud in front of everybody, and I had put in those purple patches which I had remembered from *The Red Bird* in order to make the teacher happy. The only one who knew the secret was Wakabayashi.

I turned and ran back to my house. I looked for my best fountain pen, the one my father had brought home from Germany for me. I put it into my pocket and ran over to Kimura's house.

'Here! Take it, it's yours.'

'Huh?' Kimura stood in front of the family cowshed; and, backing slightly away, he looked craftily from my sweat covered face to the pen.

'What do you mean "Huh?" Do you want it or not? It's a good pen isn't it?'

'Well. . . . If that's the way you want it. . . . I'll take it.'

'Okay, but first listen. Don't tell anybody I gave it to you, see. Nobody in your family. No teacher, see. Nobody, you understand, nobody!'

As I walked through the onion fields on my way back

home, I was thinking that at last I had escaped from the one who for over six months had made me feel humiliated – from the mockery on the face of that boy.

As though nothing had happened, the grasshoppers went on complaining loudly in the weeds. The ice candy man had stopped his cart and was urinating by the side of the path. My heart was blank and empty. There was not the least trace of exultancy. The joy and satisfaction which come from doing a good deed – not the faintest hint of anything like this welled up in my heart.

I am not the only one who had such thoughts in his boyhood. You, too, were probably much the same, however different the form your thoughts took. But to keep on thinking in this way, to have thoughts like those which follow – perhaps this is something peculiar to me. Or is it that you, too, also have experiences like these hidden within your heart?

The school which I entered next was a middle school on the eastern edge of Kobe. It was one of those schools which long before had confused the aim of education with the tangible achievement of getting a high percentage of its pupils through the entrance examinations to the first rank universities. And so, dressed in our distinctive khaki uniforms, we did nothing for five years but wrestle for all we were worth everyday with drills and other preparatory study for the entrance examinations. Each class was divided into three sections, A, B, and C, according to aptitude, and the class designation stamped on the collar insignia we wore, marking us as irrevocably as convicts. In this school I sank to the average level of an uncelebrated pupil of the B group. It wasn't that I neglected my studies to any great extent, but rather that the boys around me, unlike the farmers' sons of Rokko, were all from the same sort of environment as mine; and like me they were able to see through the teachers and size up those around them.

My father was a doctor. So I, too, decided to become a doctor. I wasn't motivated by any enthusiasm or idealism. Rather, from childhood on, I had had the conviction that as far as the surest way of always having enough to eat was concerned, the best course was to become a doctor. Then, too, as my father had told me, when it was time for my military service examination, classification as a medical student would be beneficial.

In my pre-medical studies, I found natural history the most interesting subject. I spoke before about the butterfly collection and Kimura. And even after I had entered middle school, I got my greatest joy from collecting insects, injecting them with anaesthetic, and putting them in a container smelling of naphthalene.

The natural history teacher's nickname was *Okoze*, tiger fish, because with the jutting bones of his forehead and cheeks he looked like a tiger fish. He stood before us in his baggy-kneed, worn out suit; and, blinking his small eyes, he told us how he had devoted his whole life to studying the insects in the neighbourhood of Mt Rokko. I was a fourth year student at this time. After he had given a lecture describing the varieties of butterflies which were found in the Osaka-Kobe area, he brought from the specimen room a small glass case wrapped in a carrying cloth.

'Now this, you see. This I caught a year ago near the upper stream of the Ashiya River.'

Blinking proudly, he held up the glass case in his thin hands and looked around at our faces.

I had never seen such a strange butterfly. The huge wings taut like a curved bow, the soft, richly swelling body – both seemed to gleam with a silvery sheen. There were only two antennae, white as threads of raw silk. Somehow the thought stirred in me of a beautiful young dancing girl, white feathers in her hair and silver powder covering her body, one leg lightly poised, about to leap into the air.

'A mutation, you see, of course. But even though a freak, beautiful. Doctor Matsuzaki of Kyoto Imperial University said "Give it to me!" but I wouldn't hand it over.'

As he spoke, Okoze caressed the glass case with sad restraint, over and over again.

All that afternoon that silver butterfly kept flashing through my thoughts. I heard almost nothing that was said during the classes. I felt something very much like lust. I wanted to have the pleasure of inserting a hypodermic needle into that soft, silver gleaming body.

As usual, once classes were over, I went out through the gate of the schoolyard with a friend. But just at that moment, I remembered that I had left my lunch box in the classroom, and this with no conscious duplicity. I went back alone to the classroom. The afternoon sun poured over the dusty, deserted desks and benches and spilled on to the floor. The corridors were still. My footsteps turned towards the natural history specimen room. I pushed the door and found that it was not locked. By some extra-ordinary chance, frightening though it was, the circum-stances were just right. In the naphthalene-smelling room, the setting sun shone upon the glass shelves on which were arranged in proper order the cases containing all sorts of rocks, plants, and insects. I stared at the small box in the corner wrapped in Okoze's black carrying cloth. Quickly I picked it up, threw the black cloth on the floor, and thrust the case inside my canvas book bag. No one could have seen me. I stealthily opened the door again and went out into the hall, which just as before, was completely deserted.

115

When I came to school the next day, the boys in my class were talking about something in whispers.

'Poor old Okoze. Somebody made off with his butterfly.'

'No kidding! Somebody took it?'

I felt my face stiffen despite myself, and I looked away.

'But they got the guy that did it.'

'Who?'

'Yamaguchi in C. The janitor saw him going out of the door of the natural history room after class.'

Yamaguchi's little monkey face flashed across my mind. He was in the C class, the least apt group in the school. He had won for himself the undisputed reputation of class clown and the contemptuous popularity that went with it. It was Yamaguchi they said.

'They got the butterfly back then?'

'No, no. It looks as if he lost it somewhere. What an idiot he is!'

'A real idiot!'

All day long I kept looking out of the classroom window to the playground where the pathetic figure of Yamaguchi stood. Each time I stole a look, I had to catch my breath. There he was taking my punishment for me. Why hadn't he denied everything to the teachers? By afternoon it looked as though he was worn out. He was slumping, his shoulders sagging.

'So what! An idiot like him. Why did he go there if he didn't want to steal something?' To ease my conscience, I put together a theory. 'He's an idiot. So he let himself get caught. If he hadn't got caught, he would've got away with it like me.'

That day when I got home from school, I took the butterfly out of its case, and I started a fire in the garden. From the wings, which flared up and burnt like paper, a trace of silver powder brushed off and, caught in the breeze and

116

scattered, was gone in a moment. That night in bed, I felt a sharp pain in a tooth on the right side of my jaw. The weary figure of Yamaguchi returned again and again in my dreams.

The next day, nursing a swollen cheek, I came to school. In front of the gate, I saw him standing surrounded by a number of his friends, all talking and laughing about something. At once I began to walk more slowly.

'Boy! What a stunt to pull!'

After I had passed, I could still hear their voices behind me. For a day at least, it looked as if Yamaguchi was going to be treated as a little hero by C class. And he was playing the role gladly, explaining proudly with body movements and gestures.

'Old Okoze! He all but broke down! Boy, it was really funny!'

'Hey, Yamaguchi! Whatcha do with the butterfly?'

'The butterfly? Aw, I threw that inna ditch.'

Wonderfully enough, the instant I overheard these words, all that I had suffered since the day before from the pangs of conscience – my shortness of breath, my worries – all vanished with dazzling rapidity. Even more strange, my toothache itself was eased. If this was how things were, I thought, then I hadn't burnt up that silver butterfly after all. So just as on the day before yesterday and all the days previously I again sat relaxed in class, taking notes, my only worry being that I had forgotten to bring my gym kit to school.

No matter how you choose to record such experiences, you can never attain objectivity. You'll always blend in some shade of difference. Sorting through experiences like

117

these of my childhood and early youth, one could line them up any number of ways. All I've done, in fact, is to select one or two incidents which stand out most vividly in my mind.

Despite what I've written, I didn't think of myself as a person whose conscience had long been paralyzed. For me the pangs of conscience, as I've said before, were from childhood equivalent to the fear of disapproval in the eyes of others – fear of the punishment which society could bring to bear. Of course, I didn't think I was a saint, but I felt every friend I had was just like me under the skin. Perhaps it was no more than a stroke of luck or an unbroken series of them, but it so happened that nothing I ever did seemed to merit punishment; that is, my actions never brought down upon me the censure of society.

For example there's a stigma attached to adultery. When I was studying science at Naniwa High School in Osaka, I committed this sin. But even so, the experience did not leave scars, nor was I brought to task for it; instead, my life went on as tranquilly as before. As a future doctor, every day I would go to the laboratory and examine patients. I felt neither pity nor sympathy towards them, but with great complacency, I would accept their trust and hear them call me 'Doctor'.

And then, too, the time I committed adultery, I didn't appear to myself as a heartless betrayer. There was some regret, some uneasiness, some self-contempt; but as soon as I was sure that no one had ferreted out my secret, all this soon went away. My pangs of conscience, no matter how well I nurtured them, never lasted more than a month at most.

The woman I committed adultery with was my cousin.

She was five years older than I, and while she was attending a girls' academy, she had stayed for a while at our house. Perhaps she remembers well the stay with my family, but I can hardly recall the details. All that comes to mind about her as she was then is her hair plaited in two braids which hung down her back, her teeth which showed very white when she smiled, and a dimple on her right cheek. She got married as soon as she had graduated, and I didn't see her for a long time. Her husband had graduated from a private university in Osaka and worked for a wholesaler in Ozu on Lake Biwa.

But one summer when I was studying science at Naniwa High School, it suddenly occurred to me to go and visit her in Ozu. So I went and was sharply disillusioned. She had turned into a woman worn down by the world. She had been married for less than two years, but from her fatigued expression she seemed like one utterly careworn and oppressed by life. The little three-room house, perhaps because it was close to the lake, was filled with a dampness which made the reek from the toilet even more oppressive. Her husband was a man with sunken eyes, a spiritless white-collar worker.

Since there was nothing else to do, I went swimming in the afternoon; and in the evening, putting up as best I could with the incense supposed to repel mosquitoes, I had no choice but to leaf through some old magazines or to open the textbooks I had brought along. On the other side of the panel, I could hear my cousin and her husband arguing in low voices. My cousin was berating her unresourceful husband mercilessly.

'Why don't you show some spirit! If you leave that place, can't you get a job somewhere else?'

'Don't talk so loud.' I could hear the husband's quiet, suppressed voice just as distinctly as hers. 'He'll hear us.'

119

And I could also hear their interspersed coughs and tea-sipping as well.

'I'm fed up. I'm just fed up.'

After the husband had gone to work the next morning, my cousin thumped down cross-legged on the mat, sighed deeply, and began brushing up her straggly hair.

'What a life! It just doesn't pay for a girl to get married as soon as she's out of school.'

'But he's not a bad fellow really, is he?' I replied with less frankness than I might.

I had determined the day before to leave at the earliest opportunity. That night my cousin's husband had to stay overnight at his office and did not come home. After we had finished a melancholy supper, there was nothing more for the two of us to do. So until about ten o'clock, I was treated to a long recital of my cousin's complaints. Then in the middle of the night, I heard her crying. The night echoed with the sound of lapping waves from the lake, and the humidity was especially oppressive.

'Tsuyoshi, could you come here please?' I heard my cousin's somewhat strained voice. 'I've got an awful headache.'

I could never have imagined that the thing to which my curiosity and desire had been directed for so long would turn out to be such a dreary, empty experience.

'Don't tell anybody. If you promise not to, go ahead.'

So without passion, without exultation, my virginity came to an end.

The next morning the husband, his face weary, came home.

'Tsuyoshi, your bus will be here soon.' My cousin hurried me on my way. I noticed little wrinkles of pain between her eyebrows.

'Jiro, Tsuyoshi's going now.'

So, carrying my book bag, I left their house. The lake water was black and dirty, with rubber shoes and fragments of wood floating on its surface. As I walked along the shore of the lake, I felt nothing special, neither excitement, nor depression. I knew my cousin would never speak of what had happened the night before. As long as she held her husband in contempt she was never going to make any confessions of wrongdoing to him. I was at ease, then, knowing that the secret was never going to come to light.

'Having to stay at a dirty little place like that! Last night was just a partial compensation,' I muttered. I felt that there hadn't been any profit for me in it at all. I wasn't troubled by any thoughts about being a nasty fellow who for his whole life would live as one who had betrayed another man. In fact when the husband's sunken-eyed face occurred to me, I felt nothing but contempt for him.

So this was my act of adultery. The cousin now is the mother of two children. I have no idea whether or not she suffers any pangs of conscience on account of that night. In all probability she doesn't. But at any rate up to this day, she hasn't said a word about it to her husband, so he still knows nothing about it and thanks to his ignorance, she holds her place today in society as a wife and mother, as I hold mine as a simple intern.

But it isn't just a matter of adultery, nor just a matter of having a deficient sense of sin. My callousness extends to another area. Today it's probably necessary to tell you all about this too. To put it quite bluntly, I am able to remain quite undisturbed in the face of someone else's terrible suffering and death. My life as a medical student has for some years brought me into the midst of suffering on a large scale. I've seen people die in their beds, and I've seen them die under a surgeon's knife. If they turned their faces towards me, it did them no good.

'Doctor! Please! Give me a shot of anaesthetic.'

Patients who had been operated on for tuberculosis would groan unremittingly; and although their families, unable to bear it any longer, would plead with me tearfully, I was able to shake my head. 'No, any more anaesthetic would be extremely dangerous,' I would say; but what I was actually thinking was how troublesome and inconsiderate these patients and their families could be.

A patient would die. The parents and the sisters would wail; and I would put on a sad, sympathetic expression. But once out in the corridor, the spectacle would pass out of my mind. It seems as though being in the hospital, through the attrition of ordinary daily life as an intern, any sympathy or pity that I might have felt towards these people was worn down to the point where it vanished.

My lack of any urgent sense of responsibility for Mitsu Sano – was that its cause? Mitsu was the maid who took care of my room when I lived in the Yakuin section of Fukuoka. She was a girl from Saga Prefecture, in Western Kyushu. I, a third year medical student then, rented a little house just for the two of us. Her parents had died when she was very young, and her family consisted only of a sister and an older brother. One day, to my dismay, I heard Mitsu vomiting in the washroom. What flashed through my mind was not a feeling of concern that I had marked this girl for life but rather that there would be hell to pay if a baby were born.

I still remember vividly what took place that night. If there had been the least slip-up, it would have very likely been a matter of killing the girl, so dangerous was the method. Under some pretext or other, I borrowed the necessary instruments from a friend studying obstetrics, and with my own hands, I scraped out the foetus. To see what I was doing, I had nothing to depend upon but one flashlight. And so with sweat pouring off me, I pulled out the small, bloody lump of flesh. The intention foremost in my mind was never to let anyone know about this unhappy miscalculation, not to have my whole life ruined because of a girl like this. The spectacle of Mitsu suffering, as she leaned against the wall, her face drained of blood, clenching her teeth to bear the pain, touched me hardly at all. When I think of it, such a clumsy and unsanitary procedure might easily have caused peritonitis.

A month later I sent her back to her home. I moved from the rented house in Yakuin to a boarding house where I got my meals. I used the pretext of no longer needing a maid. The truth of the matter was that I couldn't bear to look at her any more. As the third class car moved away from the platform, Mitsu kept her small face pressed to the glass. It was a wet, foggy day. As the train disappeared in the mist, I must say that I breathed a sigh of relief. Then as I reflected a bit upon Mitsu's suffering, sitting there with her face pressed to the window, 'I've done something bad' was the thought that came to me. Nevertheless, the remorse was not especially acute.

Beyond this, it would be well to write something further. I've stressed this point before: I am not writing about these experiences as one driven to do so by his conscience. The affair of the composition, the stealing of the butterfly and letting Yamaguchi take the blame, the adultery with my cousin, the affair of Mitsu – all these memories are distasteful to me. But looking upon them as distasteful and suffering because of them are two different matters.

Then why do I bother writing? Because I'm strangely ill at ease. I, who fear only the eyes of others and the punishment of society, and whose fears disappear when I am secure from these, am now disturbed.

To say 'disturbed' is perhaps to exaggerate. To say 'feel

strange' would probably be nearer the mark. There is something I would like to ask you. Aren't you too, deep down, unmoved by the sufferings and death of others? Aren't we brothers under the skin perhaps? Haven't you, too, lived your life up to now without excessive self-recrimination and shame? And then someday doesn't there stir in you, too, the thought that you're a bit 'strange'?

For me this happened on a day at the beginning of this winter. From the roof of the hospital I was idly watching the B-29s bomb Fukuoka. Suguro and I were wardens, and our duty was to go to the roof during air raids. The attack that day was a fierce one. In no time at all white smoke was pouring up from every section of Fukuoka, and where it thinned we could see the flames spurting up. One group of B-29s circled the sky overhead for a full half-hour before heading back out to sea. And in the west the second formation appeared, like so many scattered poppy seeds. And when they were gone, a third group came in. The town hall, the prefectural government headquarters, the newspaper offices, the department store were all, one by one, enveloped in smoke and flames. It seemed to be happening so close to us that we could reach out and touch it.

When sunset came, the enemy planes at last disappeared. A frightening stillness seemed to descend. The sky was a sullied, murky colour. If you strained your ears, you could hear, together with the crackle of the flames, another sound, a dull, hollow echoing sound. At first I wasn't aware of it, but gradually I began to notice it, a weird noise like that of distant moaning.

'What's that?' I asked Suguro.

'The sound of buildings collapsing, isn't it?' Then Suguro listened more carefully. 'No, that's not it. It's wind from the bomb blasts.'

But if it had been buildings collapsing, it would have

been a much more violent sound; and if it had been wind stirred by the bombs, it wasn't likely that it would have persisted so long after the raid. There was no doubt that it was like the voices of a vast number of people groaning. To a doctor such groans were familiar: resentment, sorrow, bitterness, curses – all these elements compounded together went into a man's groans. And whatever the source of this sound, the tone was just the same.

I whispered to Suguro, 'It's the voices of those dying from the raid.'

Suguro didn't answer but just stood there, blinking his eyes.

And with that, weary of it all, I forgot about the voices. But that night as I lay in bed, the drawn out hollow moans came to my ears again. At first I thought it was the noise of the waves, since the sea was not too far away, but the clamour of the sea came from another direction.

At that instant there surged up in my mind memories of the school at Rokko, as well as the setting sun shining into the natural history room at my middle school, the weary figure of Yamaguchi standing on the playground, the morning I walked along the shore of Lake Biwa, the hot humid night I held my cousin in my arms, the eyes of Mitsu as she pressed her face to the glass of the window in the third-class car. I don't know why. I thought at that moment that one day I would be punished. I felt with a sharp insistence that one day I would have to undergo retribution for what I had done so far in my life. This was a time when each day people were being swallowed up to perish in smoke and flames. Only I, without so much as a scratch, went on living unpunished as though I had never done anything wrong – and this seemed not quite right to me. But even this thought, which persists now, is not one which brings any great pain in its wake. It seems

125

rather as something to be taken for granted, as an evident truth. And so it's there within me, as one and one make two, and two and two make four.

And that's about it. The other day when Dr Shibata and Dr Asai broached that matter to us, I sat staring into the blue flames of the charcoal brazier and thought:

'After doing this will my heart trouble me with recriminations? Will I shudder fearfully at having become a murderer? Killing a living human being. Having done this most fearful of deeds, will I suffer my whole life through?'

I looked up. Both Dr Shibata and Dr Asai had smiles on their lips. These men were, after all, no different from me. Even when the day of judgment comes, they'll fear only the punishment of the world, of society. I felt a deep, unfathomable weariness, coming from I don't know where. I snuffed out the cigarette Dr Shibata had given me and got to my feet.

'Will you take part?' he asked me.

'Yes,' I answered, my voice no more than a mutter.

3 · Three O'clock in the Afternoon

February 25th was a cloudy day on which snow threatened to fall at any moment. While brushing his teeth in the washroom of his boarding house, Suguro looked covertly at his face reflected in the mirror. His eyes were bloodshot from his cold and from lack of sleep. His face was pale and puffy, but it was in the main the same melancholy face that had looked back at him all these years before today.

126

'It's today. Today is the day.' Suguro spoke as though imparting the information to himself. But still he felt no excitement, no profound emotion stirred in him. His mind, strangely enough, seemed composed.

'Good morning.' A student who was a fellow boarder came into the washroom dressed in work clothes. 'It looks as if it's going to snow, doesn't it?'

'Yes, it does,' Suguro answered, plying his toothbrush. 'You've got volunteer work today, Takahashi?'

'The factory work is at night. I go on in the afternoon. And you, Doctor Suguro?'

'I'm leaving in a minute.'

For breakfast Suguro always ate whatever was available in the hospital dining room. And so he started for the Medical School, walking on the path, whose surface was crumpled and twisted with the pressure of the frost. As he walked along, his footsteps crunching upon the half-frozen ground, he stopped from time to time. The words that Toda had said last night in the laboratory came back to him, 'If you're thinking of refusing, then there is still time to do it.'

Right now, if he were just to turn and walk back to his boarding house. . . . He looked behind him. That would be the thing to do, he thought. But the path stretched before his eyes, shining dull silver with the frost. If he followed it, it would take him right to the main gate of the hospital.

In front of the gate he ran into Chief Nurse Oba. He knew that she, too, was to take part in the vivisection. She was dressed in *monpe*, and as she passed Suguro, she glanced quickly at him with her expressionless Noh mask but then turned her eyes away just as suddenly and, shoulders sagging slightly, kept on walking. When he opened the door of the laboratory, he found that Toda had arrived already and was sitting at his desk, his back to the door. He didn't turn round when Suguro came in, nor did he say anything to him. With an unusually grave expression, he was writing something in a notebook. The hand of the old alarm clock on the desk indicated nine o'clock. It was to begin at three in the afternoon.

All through the day up to three o'clock, Toda and Suguro hardly spoke a word. While Toda was making ward rounds, Suguro, with nothing else to do, stayed at his desk. On other days when he arrived at the laboratory, there were always all sorts of odd jobs clamouring to be attended to. Why on this day was there such a feeling of everything being settled and in order? There was nothing to be done, nothing to engage him at all, he felt, other than what was to happen at three o'clock in the afternoon. So when Toda came back to the laboratory, Suguro got up and went out into the hall, as though he had thought of something. When after a while he came back, he found that Toda had left his notebook face down on the desk and gone off somewhere. They were avoiding each other and the chance of having to exchange words.

But, finally, close to three o'clock, as Suguro was about to go out, Toda blocked his way at the door.

'Hey, why have you been avoiding me?'

'I haven't been avoiding you.'

'There's no way out. That's for sure, isn't it?'

He stared hard at Suguro's face for a few moments. Then realizing the ineptness of his own question, he gave a twisted, bitter smile. And they both stood like this before the door. There was an uncanny silence throughout the hospital wing. The patients were waiting for the end of the quiet period, no concern of theirs what was to happen within half an hour. There was not a sound from the nurses' room either.

However, when the two of them climbed the stairs to the second floor operating room a bit later, the painfully oppressive atmosphere was unexpectedly shattered. The corridor, in fact, echoed with laughter. Four or five officers, whom Suguro and Toda had never seen, were leaning against the window ledges and puffing cigarettes while telling jokes in loud voices. It was as though they were waiting to be served lunch at the Officers Club.

'It's after two-thirty, isn't it? And the prisoners aren't here yet.'

The chubby little medical officer who had been in Dr Shibata's room that day clucked his tongue, as he opened his camera case.

'According to the order they were to be taken from the compound thirty minutes before. So they ought to be here before long,' an officer sporting an under-developed moustache answered, consulting his watch.

'I think I'm going to get some good pictures today,' said the medical officer, spitting on the floor and rubbing the spot with his boot.

'You really know how to handle one of those, don't you, Sir? That's a fine camera,' said the officer with the moustache, ingratiating himself as best he might.

'Oh, the camera. It's German made. After this there's going to be a farewell party for Lieutenant Omori in the hospital dining room. They say the experiment is going to be over at five o'clock. So we made it five-thirty.'

'How about the food?'

'Well whatever else, thanks to the prisoners, we'll be able to dine on a bit of American liver.'

With not a glance in the direction of Toda and Suguro, the officers laughed uproariously. The door of the operating theatre stood open, but the Old Man and Doctor Shibata and Asai were not there yet.

'You know in China. . . .' The medical officer, scratching his buttock, began a story. 'No joke. I heard in my outfit

129

there was a bunch who opened up a chink and tried his liver.'

'They say it goes down surprisingly well,' said the officer with the moustache, his face aglow with knowing complacency.

'Well, what do you say? Let's give it a try at dinner today!'

At that moment Asai came slowly down the corridor, his rimless glasses catching the light as always. With the officers he turned on his customary charm.

'The prisoners have just come, gentlemen.' His feminine tones assured them that all was well.

'Yeah, but Shibata, where is Shibata?'

'He'll be here in a moment. No need for hurry, gentlemen.'

With that, he gestured with both hands to Suguro and Toda who were leaning against the wall as though to gain support against the oppression weighing upon them.

'Come here a minute, both of you.'

After he had called them into the operating theatre, he shut the door.

'They had to come, *that* bunch! The patients are going to sense that something is up. But anyway, first of all, the prisoners haven't been warned at all about what's going to happen. They think they were brought here to get a medical check up before being sent to the camp at Oita.' After he said this, his thin voice betraying his uneasiness, he took an ether container from the shelf. 'I want you to take care of the anaesthetic. O.K.? Today there are two prisoners. One of them has been wounded in the shoulder. With him, there'll be no trouble. We're giving him an anaesthetic in order to treat him. But it'll be awkward if we do anything to alarm the other one. So when they come, I'll pretend that I'm giving them an examination, you see.

Finally, I'll ask them to lie down on the table so that I can check their hearts.'

'We'll have to strap them down, won't we? Otherwise during the initial anaesthetic period, they're liable to start resisting.'

'Of course, of course. Suguro, you're familiar too, aren't you, with the anaesthetic stages?'

'Yes, Doctor.'

There were three stages before the patient was fully anaesthetized. Furthermore, since the patient was easily roused from this kind of anaesthetic, it was essential throughout the operation to keep a careful watch.

This was the task entrusted to Suguro and Toda.

'The Old Man and Doctor Shibata?'

'They are putting on their surgical gowns in the room below. Once the anaesthetic takes effect, I'll call them. If everybody is here from the beginning, you see, the prisoners are liable to get alarmed.'

As he listened, Suguro had the impression that there was nothing unusual about the operation he was about to take part in. It was only the word *prisoner* that jolted him out of that illusion. He found himself oppressed by the realization that he had at last come to the point where it was irrevocably a matter of going ahead or turning aside.

'We are about to kill a man.' All at once a dark wave of fear and dismay began to flood through him. He grasped the handle of the door of the operating theatre. He could hear the echoing laughter of the officers on the other side. Their laughing voices seemed to thud against Suguro's heart, to block off his way of escape, a massive, thick wall in his path. Soon the stream of water, gleaming in the light from the ceiling lamp, would begin to flow across the floor of the operating theatre, with a light trickle, ready to wash away the patient's blood. Asai and Toda took off their

131

jackets and shoes in silence and began to put on their surgical gowns and wooden sandals.

The door opened and Chief Nurse Oba, her Noh mask expression fixed as always, came in with a nurse called Ueda. The women too had a sombre air as they opened the cabinets and began to lay out the scalpels, scissors, oiled paper, and absorbent cotton, on top of the glass table next to the operating table. No one said a word. All that could be heard now were the voices of the officers talking in the corridor and the trickle of the water, which had just begun.

Suguro wondered why, besides Chief Nurse Oba, the nurse Ueda was taking part in the vivisection. She had not been at the hospital long, and Suguro had seldom had anything to do with her while making his rounds; but he had a distinct impression of her as a woman of dark mood, forever staring at something far in the distance.

Suddenly the laughter in the corridor stopped. Suguro looked to one side at Toda, his eyes fearful. Toda was Toda, and though his expression was shot through with pain for an instant, he gave a mocking smile as though in challenge.

The door of the operating theatre opened, and the officer with the under-developed moustache, who had been officiously consulting his watch before, poked his shaven head into the room.

'Is everything ready here?'

'Bring one in please,' Asai answered in a strained voice. 'How many are there? Are there two?'

'Two.'

Suguro sagged back against the wall. And then he saw a tall, thin prisoner come into the room as though he had been pushed. Just like the other prisoners Suguro had seen outside the entrance of Second Surgery, this man was dressed in a loose, ill-fitting green fatigue uniform. When

132

he looked around at Suguro and the others in their surgical gowns, he smiled in a flustered way. Then he gazed at the white walls of the room.

'Sit here.' Addressing him in English, Asai pointed to a chair; and the man, awkwardly bending his long legs, sat down trustingly.

Suguro had seen many movies starring Gary Cooper. This American prisoner – his face, his way of moving – somehow resembled the actor. When Chief Nurse Oba had taken off his jacket, Suguro saw that he was wearing a torn, Japanese made vest. Through the rips in his vest, the thick, chestnut coloured hair of his chest was visible. When Dr Asai reached for his stethoscope, the prisoner shut his eyes as though dismayed, but then suddenly he became aware of the odour which floated through the room.

'Say, that's ether, isn't it?' he exclaimed.

'That's right. It's to cure you.' As well it might, Asai's voice shook slightly, and his hand trembled as it held the stethoscope.

The patient seemed to become more relaxed as the examination progressed and followed all Asai's directions obediently. It was evident from his gentle blue eyes and the frequency of his friendly smile, that he had not the slightest misgivings about Suguro and the others. It seemed that the confidence that men have in doctors as a profession was quite enough to put the prisoner at ease. While giving him the explanation about the heart examination, Asai indicated the operating table, and the prisoner readily lay down upon it.

'The straps?' Toda quickly asked.

'In a minute, in a minute,' Asai answered keeping his voice low. 'If you do it now, it will seem funny. When the second stage comes or if there are any spasms, then do it right away.'

133

'The medical officers have asked if it's all right if they come in,' said Chief Nurse Oba, putting her head in from the anteroom.

'No, not yet. I'll let you know later. Suguro, have the anaesthetic mask ready.'

'No, I can't, Doctor Asai.' Suguro's voice was almost breaking. 'Let me go. I want to get out.'

Asai, over his rimless glasses, looked up searchingly, but he said nothing.

'I'll do it, Doctor Asai.' Taking Suguro's place, Toda put layers of oiled paper and cotton on the mask which lay on a wire screen.

When he saw this, the prisoner looked as though he were about to ask something, but Dr Asai quickly put on a smile and gestured with his hand. Then he put the mask over the prisoner's face. The liquid ether began to drip upon it. The prisoner moved his head from side to side as though trying to dislodge the mask.

'Fasten the straps! The straps!'

The two nurses, bending over, fastened the straps of the operating table to the prisoner's legs and body.

'First stage,' Nurse Ueda whispered, looking at the dial. During this stage a patient, feeling his consciousness slipping away, struggles instinctively.

'Stop the ether flow,' ordered Asai, pressing the hand of the prisoner.

A low animal-like groan began to come from beneath the mask. It was the second stage of the anaesthetic. During this stage, some patients roar angrily or sing. But this prisoner, in a voice like that of a dog howling far off, did nothing but utter drawn out, intermittent groans.

'Ueda, bring the stethoscope.'

Taking the stethoscope from Nurse Ueda, Asai hurriedly placed it upon the prisoner's hairy chest.

'Ueda, start the ether again.'

'All right, Doctor.'

'The pulse is slower.'

Asai released the prisoner's hands and they flopped back on to the operating table on either side of him. Then Asai began to examine his eyes with a flashlight the chief nurse had given him.

'No reflex in the cornea. All right, that does it. I'll go and call the Old Man and Dr Shibata.' Asai took away his stethoscope and put it into the pocket of his gown. 'Stop the ether for now. If you give too much, he'll die, and that would be awkward. Miss Oba, get all the instruments ready please.'

Casting a cold glance in Suguro's direction, he went out of the operating theatre. The two nurses went back to the anteroom and did as Asai had directed. The bluish shine from the ceiling lamp was reflected from the walls. As Suguro leaned against the wall, the transparent stream of water flowed relentlessly around his sandals. Toda stood by himself beside the prisoner on the operating table.

'Come over here.' Toda suddenly spoke in a low voice. 'You won't come and help?'

'It's no use, no use at all. I can't,' Suguro muttered. 'I . . . I should have refused before.'

'You're a fool. And what do you have to say for yourself?' Toda turned, glaring at Suguro. 'If it were a matter of refusing, yesterday or even this morning would have been time enough. But now, having come this far, you're already more than half way, Suguro.'

'Half way? What do you mean, half way?'

'You're already tarred with the same brush as the rest of us.' Toda spoke quietly. 'From now on, there's no way out, none at all.'

' "The Lord Buddha deigned one day . . . to visit one of his disciples who was sick. The disciple was suffering grievously because he was unable to pass his urine or faeces. The Lord Buddha hospitably visited him. 'Did you,' he asked, 'when you were in good health, watch beside the beds of your friends who were sick? Know that you are suffering so terribly all by yourself because you failed to care for others before. And now do you feel how sharp the pain is? When you cross to the other world, you will be tortured with pains that your heart will not be able to bear.' " '

Holding the dog-eared pages close to her face, Mitsu Abé read for the old man in the next bed, who was a charity patient. The bed was the same one in which the old lady had lain when she died a week before, on the night following the air raid. It was hardly past four; yet the ward was gloomy. Mitsu read as best she could by the faint light which came in through the windows.

'Doctor Suguro won't do his ward round today. There's an operation or something.' She laid the book down and spoke to the old man. 'Look, you ought to talk to the Doctor too, see. He did an awful lot of good for the woman who was in that bed before.'

The old man, feeling around in the bed for his teacup, listened like a child.

'She got to feeling pretty weak, you see, before her operation. That night after that big air raid, she died. And she wanted so much to live to see that boy of hers again that was off in the War somewhere.'

'That's how it is with us.' The old man, gripping his cup with both hands, answered, listlessly. 'We can't do nothing – it's all the same.'

Mitsu got out of bed and went over to the window. The wind was blowing hard in the garden, but the old workman in the boots was still at it with his shovel, digging into the black soil.

'My goodness, how long is this War going to go on?' Heaving a sigh, Mitsu muttered to no one at all: 'When will it be over?'

PART THREE

Before Dawn Breaks

1

The Old Man and Dr Shibata appeared at three o'clock, dressed in surgical gowns, their faces half-hidden by their masks. They were surrounded by the officers. The Old Man stopped for an instant at the threshold and glanced at Suguro, who was still leaning against the wall on the verge of weeping. Then he quickly looked away and walked in. Behind him, with all the power of a surging avalanche, came the officers; but even they, when they caught sight of the prisoner lying face up on the operating table, hesitated for an instant.

'Go ahead, gentlemen. Move a little further up please.' Behind them Asai smiled just a trifle ironically. 'As military gentlemen, you're surely used to the sight of bodies.'

After they did as he suggested, the officer with the under-developed moustache, still intent upon currying favour asked, 'Hey, you, is it all right to take pictures during the operation?'

'Of course, of course. We, too, are going to take some. Someone is coming from Second Surgery with an eight millimeter movie camera. The experiment is certainly an important one.'

'What's today?' Breaking in, the short fat medical officer who had left the 'bounty' in Dr Shibata's room made a gesture with his finger on his shaven head. 'Are you going to cut here?'

'No, no lobotomy. Tomorrow Doctor Kando and Doctor Arajima are going to perform that sort of experiment on another prisoner.'

'Then with you it's just the lung?'

'Yes, sir. I know there's no need to explain anything to you as a medical officer, but for the guidance of you other gentlemen, who are so kind as to take part today, I'll explain briefly what we are going to do. The experiment to be carried out on today's prisoner is a simple one. It is a matter of investigating to what degree it is possible to cut away the lung in tuberculosis surgery. That is to say, the problem of how far one may cut a man's lung without killing him is one of long duration in the treatment of tuberculosis and also has a bearing upon the practice of medicine in wartime. And so today, therefore, we intend to cut away completely one of this prisoner's lungs and the upper section of the other. That is, to put it into a nutshell. . . .'

While Asai's pleasant voice was echoing from the walls of the operating room, the Old Man stood slightly bent, staring down at the water running across the floor. His slumped shoulders had a strange, painfully sad look about them. Only Chief Nurse Oba kept an expressionless face. She took some mercurochrome over to the operating table and began to paint the side of the prisoner. The liquid stained red his strong neck and chest and the breast covered with thick chestnut-coloured hair. And further down, his white stomach, still untouched by the liquid, softly rose and fell. As Toda looked at that broad, white stomach, with the fine golden hair growing on it, he seemed for the first time to become aware that this was a white man, an American soldier taken prisoner by the Japanese.

'The bastard's sleeping peacefully, isn't he?' laughed one of the officers in the rear, perhaps with the intention of dissipating the gathering tension. 'Little does he know he'll be done for in half an hour.'

The words 'done for' reverberated hollowly inside Toda. The realization that this was an act of murder had not yet taken form in his mind. To strip a person of his clothes, lay him on an operating table, give him ether – all this he had done to patients countless times, from his student days up to the present. Today it was the same. In a moment the Old Man would in a low voice call for the formal bow to the patient, and the operation would begin. There would be the metallic clicking noise of the scissors and tweezers and the dry crackling sound which accompanied the electric scalpel, and the Old Man would begin to cut in a line describing an ellipse on that chest covered with chestnut hair. What was the difference between this and other operations? The brilliant bluish white glare from the ceiling lamp and the white figures in surgical gowns moving slowly about in it with the gentle rhythm of floating seaweed had become familiar to him over the years. The figure of the prisoner lying with his face towards the ceiling differed in no way from that of ordinary patients. The prickly sensation of being about to murder someone did not stir at all in Toda. He felt that all would be brought automatically to a proper conclusion. With a certain sluggishness, he inserted the long, thin catheter tube into the prisoner's nostrils. The nose was long with a reddish tip, the nose of a white man. All Toda had to do was to adjust the nozzle of the oxygen machine to complete the preparations. The ether seemed to have taken full effect. The prisoner was sleeping, a slight snore coming through the tube. Thick leather straps firmly bound his legs in the green fatigue trousers and both his hands. Oblivious to the gaze of those around him, he faced upwards towards the ceiling. This expression was so relaxed that it looked almost as though a faint smile were playing about his lips.

'We should get started, eh, Doctor?' Dr Shibata asked the Old Man after checking the blood pressure gauge.

143

The Old Man, who had been staring at the floor, gave a start as he heard the question.

'We're going to get started.' Asai spoke sharply. The atmosphere was so hushed that the sound of swallowing which followed could be heard distinctly.

'The vivisection is beginning at 3.08 pm. Toda, put that in the record.'

The Old Man took the electric scalpel in his hand and bent over the prisoner. Toda could hear the dull whir of the movie camera behind him. Dr Arajima of Second Surgery had started to record the vivisection process. At the same moment with startling abruptness, a chorus of throat clearing coughs and snuffles arose from the officers.

As he looked at the blood pressure gauge, Toda felt a strange thought pressing in upon him, 'I'm going to be in this film too. Think of it! I've just checked the gauge. My head moved. The movement of a person, of me, of me engaged in the murder of a human being. My actions are going on to that film down to the last detail. The actions of a murderer. Afterwards, when the film is shown, will it rouse any special emotions in me?'

Toda felt an unaccountable disillusionment and fatigue. He had expected this moment, but he had hoped for a more lively fear, a keener heartache, a violent self-accusation. But the sound of the water flowing over the floor, the crackling echo of the electric scalpel – these were merely dull and monotonous and strangely sad. There was lacking even the usual atmosphere of tense concern – the worry about the patient being threatened with shock, his pulse becoming too rapid, his breathing changing abruptly. Everyone knew that this man was to die. There was no reason at all to prolong his life. So the movements of the Old Man holding the electric scalpel, of Asai, who assisted him, of Shibata, who stood by, of Chief Nurse Oba, who took care of the instruments and gauze – all of them had a certain perfunctory and sluggish quality.

The whirring of the eight millimeter camera went on as before, blending with the noise of the electric scalpel and of the scissors.

'What is Arajima thinking as he takes his pictures?' Toda wondered. 'Where did I hear that sound before? That's it! The sound of cicadas. I heard it the time I went to my cousin's house in Ozu, when I was going to summer school at Naniwa. Why am I thinking now of the damned foolish thing I did then?'

He turned his head and stole a glance at the officers gathered behind him. On the edge of the group, one young officer with glasses had turned his head away, his face like wax. It seemed that the first graphic sight of the innards of a living man was a bit more than he had bargained for. But when he became aware of Toda's glance, he straightened up and frowned.

Beside him, the officer with the moustache stood with his mouth foolishly agape and his face glowing with sweat. He stood behind the fat medical officer, craning his neck to peer over his head and licking his lips again and again, as though intent on missing not a moment of the spectacle unfolding before him.

'Silly bastards,' muttered Toda to himself. 'What silly bastards!'

But why, and what he himself was, Toda did not have sufficient energy to speculate upon. To think at all required too much effort. The warmth of the operating theatre was enough in itself to make one feel faint. The sultry air oppressed him and Toda found himself unable to concentrate upon what he was to do.

The prisoner on the table began to cough violently. The secretion was flowing into his bronchial tubes. Asai reached for the anaesthetic mask, and Toda heard him question the Old Man.

'Should I use cocaine?'

'No need.' Suddenly the Old Man straightened up from the operating table and spoke in a voice choked with anger, 'He's no patient.'

His furious tone disconcerted everyone, and the silence of the operating theatre deepened. Only the dull, drawn out whir of the camera continued unabated.

In front of him, as he leaned against the wall, Suguro saw the backs of the officers. From time to time they would clear their throats or shuffle their feet as they felt the pinch of numbness. Often at such times, a space would open briefly between two of them, and Suguro would catch a fleeting glimpse of the Old Man and Dr Shibata bent over the operating table and of the patient in his green fatigue trousers bound to the table by leather straps.

'Scalpel.'

'Gauze.'

'Scalpel.'

Dr Shibata directed Chief Nurse Oba in a hoarse voice.

'Next,' Suguro thought, 'it'll be the raspatory and cutting the rib bone.'

As an intern, he could tell just from Dr Shibata's commands where the Old Man was cutting on the prisoner's body and could picture exactly what was occurring.

Suguro shut his eyes. He shut his eyes and tried to think that he was not really involved in a vivisection being performed on a prisoner but that this was a routine operation performed on a regular patient. He tried to force his imagination: 'Let's help the patient. Let's get busy. Give a camphor shot. Supply some fresh blood.' His mind worked. 'There's Oba's footsteps. She's going to give the patient some oxygen.'

146

But then there was the dull sound of a rib bone snapping and, a moment later, the lighter sound of it dropping into the receptacle echoing from the walls of the operating theatre. The ether had been cut off perhaps. The prisoner suddenly let out a low pitched groan.

The pounding in Suguro's chest, the whispering within him increased in tempo: 'To help, to help!'

Suddenly the scene of Mrs Tabé's operation surged up in his mind. That morning all those standing around the table on which her body lay, ripped and torn like a pomegranate, drew back towards the wall, their faces taut. The only sound then had been the faint trickle of the stream of water flowing over the floor under the glare of the ceiling lamp. It had been Chief Nurse Oba who had brought the dead body, as though still alive, back to the room.

'The operation was successful.' The feigned smile on his face, Dr Asai had spoken to the mother and sister in a dark corner of the corridor.

'Not to help?'

Suguro suddenly felt a rush of shameful futility blocking his chest with such intensity that it choked his breathing. What he could do would be to lift his hands and knock aside the shoulders of the officers lined up before him. He could snatch the raspatory from the Old Man's hand. But when he looked he saw the stern shoulders of the officers packed together in a broad mass. Hanging at their sides, their swords shone with a leaden dullness. One young officer happened to turn and, seeing Suguro standing behind them dressed in a surgical gown, looked at him suspiciously. The look became an angry, accusing one.

'What's the matter with you, afraid?' those eyes asked. 'How can a young Japanese be so weak?'

He writhed under the officer's stare, aware of what he seemed: a doctor unable to carry out his duties – and

147

aware too of what he really was: a spineless coward who had been unable to refuse Dr Shibata.

'I can't do anything at all,' he groaned, looking towards the figure in green fatigue trousers on the operating table. 'I can't do anything for you.'

At that moment Asai's voice echoed sharply: 'The prisoner's left lung has been removed entirely. Now the excision of the upper section of the right lung is in process. In experiments performed up to now, when half of both lungs together have been excised, the result has been instant death.'

Then the officers' boots began to make an unpleasant squeaking sound. At some time or other, the noise made by Arajima's camera had stopped, and now the only sound that spread through the room was that of the light flow of water.

'Forty . . . thirty-five . . . thirty.' Toda was reading the blood pressure gauge. 'Thirty . . . twenty-five . . . twenty . . . fifteen . . . ten. That's it. It's over.'

After he had relayed this information to the Old Man and Dr Shibata as his job demanded, Toda slowly straightened up. For a few moments the silence continued; but at last, like a dam bursting, the officers began to cough and scrape their boots.

'So it's done!' The fat medical officer standing in the front row wiped the sweat from his head with a handkerchief. 'What was the time?'

'4:28,' Asai answered. 'The operation began at 3:08; therefore the time taken was one hour and twenty minutes.'

The Old Man looked down at the corpse, not saying a word. His gloved hands, gleaming with smeared blood under the ceiling light, still tightly gripped the scalpel. As though to thrust him out of the way, Chief Nurse Oba pushed herself between him and the table and covered the

148

corpse with a white sheet. Staggering slightly, the Old Man retreated two or three steps, but he still just stood there, without making a move.

When the officers had opened the door of the operating theatre and gone out into the corridor, the weak afternoon sun was shining through the windows. Looking out of a window, the officers stood for a time rubbing their eyes, twisting their necks with annoyed expressions, massaging their shoulders, and affecting wide yawns.

'Nothing special at all,' one suddenly offered in a voice which, as he had intended, echoed loudly from the walls.

'Lieutenant Murai, your face – you look as if you've just had a woman!'

The speaker pointed a finger at the eyes of his companion, his taunting voice not without a touch of wonder. 'Your eyes are all red.'

But it was not just he whose eyes were red. Actually, all of them had faces flushed with blood and covered with sweat – the sort of look which follows upon sexual consummation.

'It's the truth. A face just as if you'd slept with a woman.'

'Is that so? Well, I've got an awful headache too.'

'Lieutenant Omori's farewell party's at five-thirty. Let's get some fresh air.'

Their footsteps clattered noisily as the officers went down the staircase.

When they had gone, Chief Nurse Oba cautiously put her head out into the corridor. When she had made sure that no one was around, she and Miss Ueda wheeled out the trolley bearing the thing covered with the white sheet. Suguro, who had come into the anteroom, watched them as he supported himself against the wall. The squeaking of the trolley seemed to exert a fascination upon him. The sound would stop and then recur from time to time until

149

it ceased completely after the trolley had disappeared down the long, deserted corridor, whose floor shone dully in the pale sunlight.

Where he should go he didn't know. What he should do, he didn't know. The Old Man, Asai, Shibata and Toda were still in the operating theatre, but Suguro could not go back in there.

'Killed him . . . killed him . . . killed him . . . killed him. . . .' In his ears someone's voice was chanting with a formless rhythm.

'I didn't do anything at all.' Suguro made an effort to shut out the voice. 'I didn't do anything at all.' But this plea seemed to reverberate within him, churning itself into a whirlpool devoid of meaning.

'That's it! You've hit it there! You didn't do anything at all. The time the old lady died, this time too – you didn't do anything at all. You're always there. You're always there – not doing anything at all!'

As he walked down the staircase, his footsteps sounding in his ears, the thought came to him that just two hours before, the American soldier, suspecting nothing at all, had climbed these same stairs. At this he saw clearly once more the figure of the American prisoner with a desperate expression on his face. Then there was the abrupt image of Chief Nurse Oba roughly throwing a sheet over the slashed, bloody flesh.

He felt his throat violently constricted by the urge to vomit. He leaned against the window and told himself that he should have become used to seeing bloody flesh, considering his experience which stretched back to the beginning of medical school. But, still, the colour of that blood, the colour of that flesh differed from what he had seen in all previous operations over that long period. But was it the colour of the flesh and blood that provoked the nausea in

150

him, or was it the thought of the ugly brutality of Chief Nurse Oba's action?

Outside the window, the wires leading from a transmission station hummed in the cold afternoon air. Two or three birds flew across the overcast winter sky. Smoke climbed slowly from the stack of the sterilization unit. From the distant back entrance a work-party of nurses were returning, dragging their shovels and carrying their baskets wearily. Everything was just as yesterday, just as the day before, the ordinary scene about the hospital on a winter's evening. Leaning on the window sill, he waited for a second surge of nausea to pass. Then, with dragging footsteps, he went down the staircase.

He didn't see the officers in the garden. The nurses who had returned by the rear gate had laid their baskets on the lawn and now, wiping their faces with towels, were coming in his direction.

Instinctively he tried to avert his face and hurry past them as though he were fleeing. But one of them, who had sat down on a rock to rest, called out cheerfully to him: 'Doctor, won't the chief surgeon make his ward rounds today either?'

Suguro didn't answer. 'It's nothing,' he thought. 'There's nothing to worry about. These nurses don't know anything. Why am I trying to hide?'

'Doctor, are you going to come?'

'Yes, I'll be there,' he finally was able to say.

'She's right. All day the thought of the ward rounds never crossed my mind at all. But right now if I go into the wards, what then? To talk to the patients as though nothing at all had happened, to take X-rays, to fill out examination charts. . . . Tomorrow, again I'll live my intern's life. With the Old Man, with Dr Shibata, with Dr Asai, and Toda. Will I be able to make the rounds just as before? Will I examine the outgoing patients? Is all this possible? Will the pleasant face of that blond-haired prisoner never stare up at me out of their faces? I can't do it. I can't forget.'

He looked down at the ground, and in some grey furrows cut in the earth he saw the severed roots of the poplar. It had been cut down at last, the job that had taken the old workman so long to accomplish was finished. Suguro gazed vacantly at the stumps. Suddenly he thought of the old lady – the old lady carried out beneath the falling rain inside a wooden crate. The poplar tree was gone. The old lady too was gone.

'I'm not going back to the laboratory. I'm quitting.' Then he whispered to himself, 'You've ruined your life.'

But was it only him? Couldn't the same be said about everyone? He didn't know.

2

When Toda, the last to leave, was coming out of the operating theatre Asai was waiting in the corridor, holding a receptacle of the kind used during operations. It was wrapped in gauze. He was smiling.

'Toda, wait a minute. Would you bring this up to the conference room for me?'

'Yes, Doctor.'

'The military gentlemen are having a farewell party up there.'

'What is this?'

'Something Medical Officer Tanaka ordered. It's the prisoner's liver.'

Asai lifted the gauze and handed the container to Toda. A dark brown mass of flesh was soaking in a thick liquid stained dark red with blood.

'What's the idea?'

'It can be pickled in alcohol, maybe, and make a good souvenir,' Asai answered in a brisk tone. His voice was just as composed as it was at other times, as when, after finishing an autopsy or something similar, he turned to the next order of business.

As Toda dropped his gaze to the slippery mass of flesh, he could clearly visualize the broad white stomach of the prisoner, as he lay face up on the operating table. The stomach which had glistened with an almost glaring whiteness when Chief Nurse Oba was applying the mercurochrome. He was gone now. He wasn't anywhere at all. Not anywhere at all – but here in this heavy lump soaking in this clogged, dark red liquid. Was that the truth of it? He felt a weird sensation pressing upon him, as though all this were a dream. That broad white stomach, this dull brown chunk of flesh – he could not reconcile them; and his incomprehension held him for a few moments in a sort of stupor.

'Not much to it, is there?' Asai whispered softly all at once. 'We've all got used to looking at corpses, but sentimentality is never too far off.'

Quietly, Toda raised his eyes and stole a look at Asai's face. The rimless glasses had slipped down his nose. Nothing had altered in it. It was the face of the man who had a special talent for tossing sweet, comforting words to patients during ward rounds. The face of the man who would appear in the laboratory whistling and who would cluck his tongue as he ran through the examination charts.

153

There was no trace upon it of his having killed a man just a short time before.

'And *my* face is the same.' The thought was painful to Toda. 'Nothing is changed. My heart is tranquil. The pangs of conscience, the stabs of guilt that I've waited for so long haven't come at all. No dread at having torn away someone's life. Why not? Why is my heart so devoid of life?'

'Toda.' Asai, the enigmatic smile still on his face, pressed the other's arm, which was holding the receptacle. 'There's something I've got to talk to you about. Afterwards, have you thought about staying on here at the University?'

'At the University?'

'Yes, as an assistant. Doctor Shibata said something about it recently. So if you happen to be willing. . . .'

'Well, I don't know. There are other people better qualified than I,' Toda answered, looking down, sensing that there was something behind Asai's words. 'There's Suguro.'

'No, not Suguro. He's hopeless. Toda, about him. Today, just at the critical time, where did he go to?'

'He was there in the operating theatre. I'm sure he was watching from the back.'

'He won't say anything, that fellow, I hope.' All at once Asai's face came very close, an uneasy expression on it. 'If there is the least chance of anything leaking out. . . .'

'Don't worry about him. He just can't take it, that's all.'

'If that's so, I feel better. Well, anyway, think over what I said, will you? The Old Man too – he doesn't have what it takes any more. From now on, Dr Shibata and I together plan to get First Surgery on its feet again. If you'd like to join in, such a matter as your recommendation as assistant will be a mere trifle. Then too – something to bear in mind – with regard to today's matter: from now on we are going to have to stick close together. We're all in just as deep, you see.'

When Asai had disappeared down the deserted corridor, Toda, still holding the container, felt a deep, all pervading fatigue.

' "To stick close together," he says. He wants to make use of the accomplice spirit to draw me in and prevent any whisper of the affair leaking out. As though I couldn't see what he's up to: dangling attractive bait in front of me in order to make his own position solid in First Surgery. That bastard Asai. What does he think about the chunk of flesh here, I wonder?'

The prisoner who had been alive just two hours ago, a tense look in his brown eyes – had Asai already forgotten all about his death? Immediately after stepping out of the operating theatre, he was quite capable of neatly tying up every loose end to secure his own future. Toda marvelled at this remarkable ability to sort things out so coolly.

'But what do I think, me, who am holding this right now, this bucket with the flesh in it? This drab brown lump pickled in dark red liquid. What I'm afraid of isn't this. My heart is so odd that I feel nothing, no pain at all when I look at something that was part of a man whom I murdered.'

He pushed open the thick, heavy door of the conference room with his shoulder. Three or four officers turned in his direction. They had removed their jackets and were sitting beside a table upon which saké cups and other tableware had been laid out, warming their hands over a charcoal brazier.

'Is Medical Officer Tanaka here?'

'He'll be here soon. What do you want?'

'It's something which he ordered.'

'Thanks.'

155

One officer got up. He was the man whose face had been as pale as wax throughout the operation. When he had pulled aside the gauze and looked inside, his face became painfully contorted.

'What is it, Lieutenant Ebara?'

'It's the prisoner's liver,' said Toda. And having duly fulfilled his assigned task, he turned and walked out of the silent room.

After he shut the door of the conference room, the floor of the long corridor, with its dull leaden shine, stretched out before Toda. There was no one to be seen. If he were to walk back straight along this corridor, he would be at the door of the operating theatre once again. As he thought about this, Toda felt churning within him a desire to go back and look at that room, an excitement which he found hard to control.

'Just once more. I want to see what will happen if I go back there after that.'

The last light of late afternoon gradually faded from the windows. It was quiet. From the conference room behind him, the low sound of voices could be heard every now and then through the door.

After descending one or two steps of the staircase, he stopped. Then he turned around abruptly and with the walls of the corridor echoing his footsteps, he walked in the direction of the operating theatre.

The door stood open a little. When he pushed it, it gave with a dull squeak. The faint smell of ether came to his nostrils. On the blank white top of the table in the preparation room, an anaesthetic bottle lay forlornly on its side.

Toda stood for a few moments in the middle of the room. Here it was, he recalled, that the prisoner had exclaimed, 'That's ether, isn't it?' The childish tone of the exclamation was still in his ears. A formless fear for a

156

moment clutched at his heart, but Toda kept his control. The fear dissolved into ripples and disappeared, leaving him an uncanny composure.

What he wanted now was a feeling of bitter self-recrimination. The sharp pang stabbing at the breast, the remorse which rips and tears at the heart. But even though he had returned to the operating theatre, no such emotions welled up within him. Unlike a layman, he had long been accustomed to entering the operating theatre alone after an operation. Those other times and now – was there any difference? If there was, he found himself unable to grasp it.

'Here we took off his fatigue jacket.' Tracing over insistently in his mind every aspect of the scene which had taken place, he waited in vain for the pain of remorse to wring his heart.

'That prisoner, he seemed as embarrassed as a woman about his chest with its blond hair. He covered it with his hands. And then, just as Asai told him to, he went into the operating theatre there.'

He softly opened the inner door. He flicked the light switch, and the ceiling lamp's bluish white glare was reflected from the walls of the room. The operating table had a slight crack on its surface. Next to this lay a small piece of gauze that had been overlooked. There was a dark stain of blood upon it. Even confronted with that, Toda felt no particular pain.

'I have no conscience, I suppose. Not just me, though. None of them feel anything at all about what they did here.'

The only emotion in his heart was a sense of having fallen as low as one can fall. He turned off the lamp and went into the hallway once more.

The corridor was already wrapped in the darkness of

157

evening. As Toda walked along, he heard the sharp echo of footsteps from the staircase towards which he was going. Someone slowly came up the stairs and turned in the direction of the operating theatre. For no particular reason, Toda stepped into a window recess and watched as a man in a white jacket approached, his figure looming up in the dark like a spectre. It was the Old Man.

Without noticing Toda, the Old Man stopped in front of the door of the operating theatre. With both hands plunged into the pockets of his coat, the Old Man, his back bent, stood facing the door, not moving. Toda could not see his face clearly, but the impression conveyed by the sagging shoulders, bent back and the white hair visible in the blackness was one of old age, weary and enervated. For a long time the Old Man stared at the door. Finally, his footsteps echoing once more, he went off in the direction of the staircase.

'Doctor, would you come to the ward for a moment please? There's a patient who's had a fever since this morning.' Suguro heard a nurse's voice behind him.

'All right,' turning his head, he answered in a low voice.

'We didn't see anything of Doctor Asai or Doctor Toda or anybody today. Was there an operation?'

'No, no operation.'

'But the chief nurse wasn't around either. All at once they sent us out to dig slit trenches. What was it anyway?'

Suguro stole a quick glance at the young nurse's face. Her expression was guileless as she awaited his answer.

'I'll come to the ward. I have to fetch my stethoscope.'

He walked into the ward; and when, from the three rows of beds looming up white before him in the gloomy shadow, he felt the concentrated gaze of the patients fasten upon him, his knees shook. Eyes cast down, he passed down the aisle in front of the beds as though running the gauntlet.

'I can't look them in the face any more,' he groaned within himself. 'And these people don't know anything about it at all.'

The patient with the fever was the old man lying in the bed next to Mitsu Abé, where the old lady had lain a month earlier. When he saw Suguro, he displayed his purplish gums almost devoid of teeth. He screwed up his face and tried and tried to express what was wrong.

'He wants to say that his spit gets stuck in his throat,' Mitsu Abé broke in. 'You'll be all right now. Just leave everything to Doctor.'

Suguro gently grasped the old man's outstreched arm. It was so emaciated that he could have easily encircled it with his thumb and forefinger. The touch of that skin covered with white splotches and rough with wrinkles made him think of the arm of the old lady.

'Please do something for him, Doctor. Please do something for him.' Blinking repeatedly, Suguro heard Mitsu Abé's faint voice at his side.

Chief Nurse Oba and Nobu Ueda slowly descended to the dark basement in the squeaking hospital elevator.

'Say, this elevator makes an awful noise. It needs greasing, don't you think?' Nobu Ueda muttered, looking up at the metal ceiling of the elevator, from which the paint had almost entirely peeled off.

But the chief nurse, leaning against the wall with her eyes shut, didn't bother to respond. Nobu thought that the chief nurse's face was gaunter than usual and her cheekbones more prominent. Nobu hadn't had a chance to study the chief nurse's face so leisurely at close range before, and she was startled to notice how much grey was mixed with the black hair that had escaped the white cap.

'Why this one is really up in years.' With ill-disposed eyes, Nobu studied the other's profile. Years ago, before her marriage, when Nobu was registered at this hospital, Chief Nurse Oba had been four years ahead of her and no more than an ordinary nurse. Now, estranged from her companions and without anyone who could be called a friend, she strode about with her expressionless face, highly prized and made much of by all the doctors, but berated by the other nurses as 'Miss Curry-favour' behind her back.

To wear a little lipstick and makeup as the other nurses did would be unthinkable for Chief Nurse Oba. Then, still more, it would be hard to imagine her dark face with its jutting bones bewitching the heart of any male patient.

'So now you're the chief nurse, eh?' Nobu whispered to herself, feeling a surge of envy and dislike for this woman who had become her superior.

When the elevator had reached the basement, Nobu grasped the handle of the trolley, which was between them, and pulled it out into the corridor. Naked light bulbs burned gloomily at forlorn intervals in the ceiling, which was lined with exposed pipes. Before the War, this section had been a place for shops and tearooms run by the hospital. Now the rooms were abandoned to the dust, used only as shelters during air raids. Since the morgue was at the far end of the corridor, Nobu began to push the trolley in that direction, but the chief nurse, who had been silent up to then, stopped her.

'The other way, Mrs Ueda.'

'But shouldn't it go there?'

'The other way.' Her expressionless face hardening, the chief nurse shook her head.

'But why, I wonder?'

160

'It doesn't matter why. Do as I say.'

She wheeled the trolley with the white sheet over it down the corridor, filled with the odour of damp cement, towards the opposite end. While she pushed the trolley, Nobu studied the thin, stubborn back of the chief nurse, who was gripping the handles at the front of the trolley.

'She's like a stone, that's what she is. No human sympathy in her at all.'

At the very thought of the blank, stony face of this woman, Nobu felt a sudden shock at her breast as though from a collision. The light from the naked bulbs, leaving dark shadows, fell upon scattered bags of cement, broken laboratory tables, and various kinds of chairs with the stuffing protruding from them. The wheels of the trolley kept up their monotonous squeak.

'Chief?' Nobu intentionally said 'Chief' instead of 'Miss Oba'. 'Before, did anyone talk to you about today?'

But her companion did not glance back. She stubbornly gripped the handles and kept moving forward. Seeing this, Nobu let an ironic smile begin to form on her lips.

'Did Doctor Asai? Doctor Asai told me all about it. Quite unexpectedly, he turned up at my apartment. Was I surprised! He had been drinking saké. Afterwards he. . . .'

'That will do, Mrs Ueda.' Chief Nurse Oba suddenly took her hands from the trolley handles. 'Stop the trolley.'

'Here? Is this all right?'

The chief nurse said nothing.

'Is someone coming to take care of it?'

'Mrs Ueda, the function of a nurse is to carry out what the doctors direct and keep her mouth shut.'

On the trolley between them, the sheet-covered corpse loomed white in the darkness. The two women stood for a moment glaring at each other with flashing eyes.

'Then, too, Mrs Ueda' – the chief nurse narrowed her

eyes – 'why don't you just take the rest of the afternoon off and go home. And there should really be no need to say this, but don't speak about today to anyone. If by chance you should be loose mouthed about this. . . .'

'If I'm loose mouthed, what'll happen then?'

'There'll be a great deal of trouble for Doctor Hashimoto. Can you understand that?'

'Is that right?' Nobu Ueda's mouth tightened. 'So we nurses can be that important to doctors, eh?'

Then as though talking to herself, she whispered loud enough for the other to hear. 'Unlike somebody else, I didn't take part today just because of Doctor Hashimoto.'

In that instant, before Nobu's eyes, pain shot through the chief nurse's face, as, her lips twisted and trembling, she tried to make some retort. From the time she had started at the hospital, Nobu had never seen the chief nurse show the least distress before a subordinate.

'Just as I thought!' Nobu's heart swelled with the joy of having at last struck the other's weak spot. 'Isn't that something! This flinty woman is in love with Doctor Hashimoto.'

Without another word to Chief Nurse Oba, she turned and, ignoring the elevator, ran out through the recently built emergency exit into the garden.

Night had already swallowed up the garden. Before the War, when she had been a nursing student, when evening came lights would be burning in the windows of the Medical School buildings and of the hospital. To her they somehow resembled ships at anchor with all their flags flying and so recalled to Nobu the harbour festivals of neighbouring Hakata, where she had once lived.

Now, however, the only lights were faint ones, those in the hospital reception room and the office. She heard the loud voices of men singing military songs. They came from

162

the second floor conference room of First Surgery. That window, too, was covered with black curtaining, but some light flickered out through an opening.

'It's the officers who were there today,' Nobu thought. 'They're really something aren't they. At a time when we've got nothing to eat but beans, they eat and drink as much as they want. I wonder what they're eating?'

Then Nobu remembered that after the vivisection was over, a fat little officer had put his mouth close to Dr Asai's ear and whispered.

'Would you cut out the prisoner's liver for me?'

'For what?'

As Dr Asai's rimless glasses flashed, the fat little officer smiled sardonically. 'The medical officers are going to have a little fun with the junior officers by having them try some of it.'

And with that, Dr Asai, too, seeing what sort of man the other was, smiled a thin sardonic smile of his own.

When Nobu recalled this exchange, she shuddered with instinctive distaste. However, apart from this passing mood, it was all one to her whether the officers ate the prisoner's liver or didn't eat the prisoner's liver. As a nurse she had grown used to operations and the sight of blood, and today the fact that the man on the operating table was an American prisoner hadn't roused any particular apprehension in her. When Dr Hashimoto cut in a straight line into the prisoner's skin, the only association of thought that this had provoked in Nobu was that of Hilda's white skin – the thought of the white hand of Hilda which had pounded the desk in the nurses' room as she fiercely scolded Nobu about the procaine injection for the patient with the spontaneous pneumothorax attack. And today, just as with Hilda's skin, faint golden hair had covered the prisoner's skin.

163

'Will Doctor Hashimoto say anything about today to Hilda, I wonder? He won't, I don't think.'

Nobu forcibly invoked within herself the sensation of having scored a joyous triumph over Hilda. 'No matter how much of a blessed saint Mrs Hilda is, she has no idea of what her own husband did today. But I know all about it.'

When she returned to her apartment, the room was completely dark. She sat down on the entrance step, suddenly overcome with weariness. She sat for some time, her shoes still on, her hands gripping her knees, staring down.

'Mrs Ueda, I put half of your soap ration by the window. Later on give me the money please.' She heard the landlord's cold voice echo down the corridor and afterwards the slam of a door.

In the darkness of her room, the whiteness of bedding and dishes strewn about shone dimly. From a radio in the house next door a warning buzzer sounded with a tearing, metallic noise.

'What'll I do now?' It was always the same. Whenever Nobu returned from the hospital to this cold room, she felt herself overwhelmed by loneliness and isolation.

'Today as usual, work is over. All over. . . .'

Yes, today as usual work was over. What she was thinking of right now was no more than that. Since she had been away from the hospital for what had seemed to her to be a terribly long time, she felt especially weary, physically and mentally. Tomorrow again it would be a matter of checking the patients' blood pressure, their saliva and all that. Mrs Hilda, all unknowing, might come to the hospital. That would be nice, she thought. And then she thought about Chief Nurse Oba.

'She's in love with Doctor Hashimoto. I'm the only one that knows that.'

She pulled off her shoes and threw them to one side and

then turned on the light, which was shaded with a wrapping cloth. She turned on the gas and put on a pan of water containing beans. She faced the usual lonely, cheerless meal. And as she always did, she took from the closet the baby clothes which she had made for Masuo. These she spread upon her lap, and, not moving, she sat for a long time looking blankly down at them.

In the darkness the tip of a lighted cigarette glowed.

'Is that you, Suguro?' Toda called in a low voice after he had come out on the roof.

'Yes.'

'*You*, smoking?'

Suguro didn't answer. He was leaning on the guard-rail, his chin in his hands, and looking straight out. Fukuoka was blacked out, prepared for an air raid. Whether there was a warning or not, when night came, not the least light would show. It seemed not as though there were lights which were hidden but rather that death had overwhelmed both lights and men.

'What are you doing?'

'Nothing.'

Then Toda became aware that Suguro was staring fixedly at the only part of the surrounding scene which was shining brightly. He was looking out at the sea. The low rumble of the black waves as they pushed in upon the sand set up a melancholy echo.

'Ward rounds tomorrow again, eh?' Yawning deliberately, Toda muttered in a sleepy voice. 'Tough, wasn't it? Today was really tough.'

Suguro put out his cigarette and turned towards Toda. Then he sat down on the concrete roof and, his arms wrapped around his knees, looked up.

165

'What is there to do?' He spoke in a weak voice. 'What are we going to do?'

'Nothing. Just do as we always do. Nothing has changed.'

'But today! Toda, it doesn't bother you at all?'

'Bother me? What do you mean, bother me?' Toda's tone was dry. 'Was it the sort of thing that should bother somebody?'

Suguro was silent. Finally as though to himself, he spoke in a still feebler voice. 'Toda, you're strong. As for me. . . . I shut my eyes today in there. I don't know what to think, even now. I just don't know.'

'What is it that gets you?' Toda felt a painful constriction forming in his throat as he spoke. 'Killing that prisoner? Thanks to him, we'll now be better at curing thousands of TB patients – because we killed him. Should we have let him live, you think? The conscience of man, is that it? It seems to vary a good deal from man to man.'

Toda raised his eyes and gazed at the black sky. Slowly, slowly he felt cutting through his heart all the old memories – of the summer vacation while at Rokko, the figure of Yamaguchi standing in the corner of playground, the sweltering night beside Lake Biwa, the bloody lump he had torn from Mitsu's womb in the rented house in Yakuin. Really there was nothing changed at all. Everything was just the same as before.

'Still . . . some day, we're going to have to answer for it,' said Suguro, leaning close suddenly and whispering. 'That's for sure. It's certain that we're going to have to answer for it.'

'Answer for it? To society? If it's only to society, it's nothing much to get worked up about.' Toda gave another obvious yawn. 'You and I happened to be here in this particular hospital in this particular era, and so we took part in a vivisection performed on a prisoner. If those

166

people who are going to judge us had been put in the same situation, would they have done anything different? So much for the punishments of society.'

Toda felt an indescribable sense of weariness and stopped talking. Explain as he might to someone like Suguro, what good would it do? A bitter surge of futility welled up within him.

'I'm going home.'

'Is that it then?' Suguro mused. 'Things are just the same with us as before?' Left alone on the roof he gazed out at the sea shining amid the blackness. He seemed to be trying to catch sight of something there.

' "When the clouds like sheep pass. . . . When the clouds like sheep pass. . . ." ' He forced himself to form the words, barely able to whisper. ' "In the sea over which moist clouds sail. . . . In the sea over which moist clouds sail. . . ." '

But he found he could not do it. His mouth was parched.

' "Sky, your scattering is white, white, / White like streams of cotton. . . ." '

Suguro could go no further. He could go no further.

New Directions Paperbooks — a partial listing

Javier Marías, All Souls
A Heart So White
Your Face Tomorrow (3 volumes)
Thomas Merton, New Seeds of Contemplation
The Way of Chuang Tzu
Henri Michaux, Selected Writings
Dunya Mikhail, Diary of a Wave Outside the Sea
Henry Miller, The Air-Conditioned Nightmare
Big Sur & The Oranges of Hieronymus Bosch
The Colossus of Maroussi
Yukio Mishima, Confessions of a Mask
Death in Midsummer
Teru Miyamoto, Kinshu: Autumn Brocade
Eugenio Montale, Selected Poems*
Vladimir Nabokov, Laughter in the Dark
Nikolai Gogol
The Real Life of Sebastian Knight
Pablo Neruda, The Captain's Verses*
Love Poems*
Residence on Earth*
Charles Olson, Selected Writings
George Oppen, New Collected Poems (with CD)
Wilfred Owen, Collected Poems
Michael Palmer, Thread
Nicanor Parra, Antipoems*
Boris Pasternak, Safe Conduct
Kenneth Patchen, The Walking-Away World
Octavio Paz, The Collected Poems 1957–1987*
A Tale of Two Gardens
Victor Pelevin, Omon Ra
Saint-John Perse, Selected Poems
Ezra Pound, The Cantos
New Selected Poems and Translations
Personae
Raymond Queneau, Exercises in Style
Qian Zhongshu, Fortress Besieged
Raja Rao, Kanthapura
Herbert Read, The Green Child
Kenneth Rexroth, Songs of Love, Moon & Wind
Written on the Sky: Poems from the Japanese
Rainer Maria Rilke
Poems from the Book of Hours
The Possibility of Being
Arthur Rimbaud, Illuminations*
A Season in Hell and The Drunken Boat*
Guillermo Rosales, The Halfway House
Evilio Rosero, The Armies
Good Offices
Joseph Roth, The Leviathan

Jerome Rothenberg, Triptych
William Saroyan
The Daring Young Man on the Flying Trapeze
Jean-Paul Sartre, Nausea
The Wall
Delmore Schwartz
In Dreams Begin Responsibilities
W. G. Sebald, The Emigrants
The Rings of Saturn
Vertigo
Aharon Shabtai, J'accuse
Hasan Shah, The Dancing Girl
C. H. Sisson, Selected Poems
Gary Snyder, Turtle Island
Muriel Spark, The Ballad of Peckham Rye
A Far Cry From Kensington
Memento Mori
George Steiner, At the New Yorker
Antonio Tabucchi, Indian Nocturne
Pereira Declares
Yoko Tawada, The Naked Eye
Dylan Thomas, A Child's Christmas in Wales
Collected Poems
Under Milk Wood
Uwe Timm, The Invention of Curried Sausage
Charles Tomlinson, Selected Poems
Tomas Tranströmer
The Great Enigma: New Collected Poems
Leonid Tsypkin, Summer in Baden-Baden
Tu Fu, Selected Poems
Frederic Tuten, The Adventures of Mao
Paul Valéry, Selected Writings
Enrique Vila-Matas, Bartleby & Co.
Elio Vittorini, Conversations in Sicily
Rosmarie Waldrop, Driven to Abstraction
Robert Walser, The Assistant
The Tanners
Eliot Weinberger, An Elemental Thing
Oranges and Peanuts for Sale
Nathanael West
Miss Lonelyhearts & The Day of the Locust
Tennessee Williams, Cat on a Hot Tin Roof
The Glass Menagerie
A Streetcar Named Desire
William Carlos Williams, In the American Grain
Paterson
Selected Poems
Spring and All
Louis Zukofsky, "A"
Anew

*BILINGUAL EDITION

For a complete listing, request a free catalog from New Directions, 80 8th Avenue, NY NY 10011
or visit us online at www.ndpublishing.com